ESSENCE

BY

ERIC DAILEY

COVER ART

BY ERIC DAILEY

St. Louis

DAILEY WORX

2014

http://www.facebook.com/DaileyWorx

daileyworx@gmail.com

TABLE OF CONTENTS

PREFACE.

In the twenty-first century technology rapidly advanced in different fields. Humanity pushed their progress in space exploration to new heights, engineering new, more efficient ways to reach further into the stars. Space elevators were built to carry massive amounts of material into space with minimal cost. Huge ships were then assembled directly in Earth's orbit. Shortly after, bases were built on the moon and in other diverse key locations across the solar system.

Mining operations arose on the moon's surface for helium 3 and other miscellaneous resources. Massive solar farms were also set in place to gather energy from the sun and beam it directly back to Earth. In the years to come many colonies grew on the surface. It became common place for numerous tourists to frequently visit the moon, either on its surface or on one of the various hotel satellites.

Shortly after the colonization of the moon began, companies started mining asteroids as well. During the beginning of asteroid mining, androids and remotely controlled computer systems were used to navigate deeper in space for longer periods of time with minimal danger to humans. Only a few short years later the Mars project began, a massive plan to terraform the planet.

Precise calculations allowed for the selection of the perfect asteroids to be taken from the kuiper belt, towed into the inner solar system and slammed into the frozen poles of the planet. This, in turn, jump started the core of the planet and the ejected debris helped scatter water into the atmosphere. Over the next several hundred years, hundreds of thousands of plants were transported to the planet from Earth, planted in the Martian soil and slowly began to fill the atmosphere with oxygen. Generations were born in the Martian colonies having never been to Earth.

During this time of human expansion across the solar system, many other professions and technologies significantly advanced as well. One company, the Takeshi Corporation, worked on several projects in genetic research in hopes of curing disease and helping enhance the human body to extend the lifespan and possibly fix damaged limbs and organs. Their lead researcher was the most distinguished scientist of his time, known as Kenji Yamato.

Around the middle of the twenty-first century the Takeshi Corporation was bought by an illusive, corrupt man under the name of Vincent Klauser. When he took control of the company, no one in the general public, or even within the company itself really knew who the owner was, with the exception of his inner circle and the top scientists. He ran his company with an iron fist and was feared by all who knew of him.

The corporation quickly switched from helping and healing research to more diabolical projects filled with secretive illegal activity. The scientists worked as Klauser's slaves, doing as he commanded, fearing for their families lives as well as their own. Sworn to secrecy, the scientists worked tirelessly in their labs. They were tasked with trying to create the next step in human evolution for the benefit of using them as soldiers.

Kenji quickly became Vincent's favorite and he used his knowledge in genetics to extend his lifespan, he also kept Kenji alive and well guarded. Kenji was tasked with cross-species gene manipulation to find ways of cellular regrowth, which would lead to regenerative capabilities and growing of lost limbs. He also worked to find ways of gaining super strength, speed, stamina and advanced cognitive abilities.

Vincent forced Kenji and his fellow scientists to do horrific experiments on human subjects and also work on human cloning research. The corporation moved to Switzerland during the twenty-second century. By this time governments were nearly non-existent. Corporations had more money, resources and power and slowly began taking control of the Earth.

As humanity's reach extended further to the stars, the Earth became over stressed by the rapid consumption of natural resources, over population and the general lack of care for the environment that the corporations and inhabitants exhibited. Over time, as Mars grew into a prosperous, fertile land, Earth grew into a more barren, desolate place. The population gathered in great mega-cities to survive, which eventually became controlled by the corporations, as the rest of the world turned to wastelands.

There were many attempts over the years by the people to fight against the corruption of the corporations. They struggled to regain control and help the Earth heal before it was too late. Unfortunately these efforts failed as the rebellion could not contend with the more advanced technology of the corporations. The rebellion was eventually scattered and the last remnants went into hiding as the population became compliant under the corporations rule.

Wars between the corporations arose for power and control. Eventually the Takeshi Corporation prevailed as the dominant power over Earth. In the years to follow, small business owners were allowed to conduct and maintain their businesses under the watchful eye of the Takeshi Corporation. They were forced to technically be owned by the corporation and pay appropriate percentages of their earnings. The Corporation maintained control over everyone, to defy them meant certain death.

Though I do not condone the use of certain actions taken in this story; to keep a realistic feel it does contain the use of violence, language, alcohol and adult situations and is not intended for children. Feel free to visit on <u>Facebook</u> and "Like" if you like the book or leave feedback, I'd love to hear your thoughts, good or bad. With your support there will be more to follow and through your feedback you will empower my stories to become better than the last.

Thanks to my daughter for being the greatest person in my life, thanks to my family and friends for being there for me when I needed them most. Thanks to my good friend James Wadlow for encouragement, allowing me to maintain enough motivation to finish this book. Thanks to Ryan Schaefer for taking time out of his busy schedule to help proof read and critique, giving me insight on the book through another person's eyes. On that note, let's jump into the story. Please read with an open mind and I hope you enjoy!

ESSENCE.

CHAPTER I.

AWAKENING.

A dark void, black as night. Through the empty nothingness comes a foggy vision of a butterfly perched on an exotic flower. Focusing behind the butterfly reveals a young child just a short distance away, as still as a statue, eyes wide as can be, intensely studying the butterfly's every move.

Her dark shoulder length hair running down along her face, chin resting on her forearm as though she's been there for hours. In her other hand she clenches a stuffed cat doll that looks as if it has never left her side.

Her clothes are as of a prestigious academy, clean and fancy with decorative buttons and a skirt, socks with lacy ruffles and black shiny shoes. The lush artificial oasis of vegetation around her is housed in a half-dome glass structure in the lobby of a research facility.

It's after hours and most of the employees have gone home to their families, except a handful of scientists, including her grandfather, working hard back in some tucked away laboratory. Rain beats down on the glass with pounding force and cracks of lightning flicker shadows across the surroundings from the raging storm outside.

She seems to be all alone in this vast facility, just her, her stuffed cat and the beautiful butterfly in front of her. Suddenly the butterfly starts to fly away and without hesitation the young girl follows, tracking it through the corridors, traveling deeper into the facility.

They pass through a tube-like hallway with an aquarium built into one of the walls, ripples from the water illuminate the surroundings from the back-lit aquarium. She slows down for a brief second, glancing in admiration at the magnificent sea life, then quickly hurries to catch up to the butterfly as it rounds a corner and heads through a slightly cracked door.

She quickly follows, paying no attention to the *Authorized Personnel Only*' sign and the door half hanging off the hinges. Inside it is hard to see, lights flickering, wreckage and debris scattered as if there was a tremendous earthquake. Broken glass from research tubes crunch as she slowly traverses the room.

She sees the flickering shadow of the butterfly flapping its wings just around the corner ahead of her and slowly approaches, holding her stuffed cat firmly against her chest, squeezing it tightly with both arms. Strange noises of low grumbling can be heard as a figure becomes somewhat visible in the shadows in the distance, hunched over, back turned.

"Grandpa?" she says in a frightened whisper, a light hanging from the ceiling flickers as it sways revealing blood trails and claw gouges on the walls.

The shadowy beast hears the child and turns toward her stepping partially into the light; a hideous, mangled creation or disastrous bi-product of the illegal research being done in the facility; holding what's left of a scientist in its left hand, blood dripping everywhere. In the reflection of her fear gaped eyes the beast lunges at her as she lets out a blood curdling scream.

The Girl gasps awake from her nightmare dripping in sweat, gripping the sheets, breathing heavily with the same frightened look on her face, yet she is no longer a child. Taking a few deep breaths she runs her fingers through her hair, locking them together as they reach the back of her neck. Leaning her head back, she opens her eyes as she takes one more deep breath and exhales.

"Mia, time?" she says as the '*My Interactive Assistant*', or 'M.I.A.', immediately responds in a female voice, "six forty two A.M."

She looks over at her stuffed cat, still as raggedy as ever, laying on the bed.

"Blinds please Mia," she asks as she stands up next to the window.

The tint changes allowing the morning sunrise over the massive city to illuminate the room.

She feels the cold touch of the glass on her fingertips as an uneasy feeling comes over her. Remembering only the past few days, this world seems hazy, unfamiliar… artificial. She is positive in her mind that the window feels cold, but is it really cold in the middle of summer?

She sees the sun rising, but feels no warmth from its rays. She stares intently out the window with her hand still on the glass. On the other side of the so-called window staring right back at her is a man in a dark room.

He overlays his hand onto hers as he gazes into her eyes, she suddenly pulls her hand away from the glass with an uncomfortable look upon her face. She picks up her cat and sits on the side of the bed, taking another deep breath as she stares at it trying to remember more. On the other side of the glass, in the dark room with the man, is another man monitoring vitals on machines while taking notes. They continue to observe her every move as she gets into the shower and prepares to start her day.

CHAPTER II.

THE HERO RETURNS.

Out of the vast empty nothingness of space; a backdrop of twinkling stars; an asteroid mining ship comes into view on its way back to Earth. Interstellar traffic picks up as the massive ship passes by the moon. The moon has been transformed into a hot spot for tourists, flashy and lit up with hotels, casinos, amusement parks and residential and mining facilities spanning across its surface.

Above its surface revolves budget hotel satellites and refueling stations with transports coming and going. As the ship approaches Earth it begins to synchronize with the Earth's orbit and comes to a halt above Europe. One of the three remaining space elevators along with a few orbiting stations can be seen glistening in the sun. Many smaller craft begin to descend out of the massive ship and head toward the surface to a handful of different areas.

A few of the smaller ships head to Zurich, Switzerland, one of the few cities left considered habitable on the surface of the over stressed Earth. The inner part of the city is built up with massive skyscrapers, amongst other structures, where the ordinary citizens and upper class go about their day. The further edges of the city become less appealing and more run down, where the less fortunate and more rebellious people maintain their own way of life. Beyond that lies a wasteland of the old world, devastated by the many harsh years of neglect by humanity and the planet's severe weather.

The ships maintain their course toward their designated landing zones; just below, a man makes his way through the run down buildings of old out of the wasteland and toward the inner city. It has been years since he stepped foot in Zurich, spending those lost years as a vagabond of the wastelands. Slung over his shoulder is an old worn bag, filled with rations and other various supplies. Along with the bag, he is also carrying his weapon of choice, an old katana, possibly the last in existence. His clothes are dirty and worn from the cruel years spent in the unforgiving wastelands. All but the long reddish overcoat he is wearing, which is very decorative and clean, except for one sleeve torn at the shoulder.

A levitating train departing the city passes in front of him at a high rate of speed, the loud horn rumbles the surroundings as it zooms by. He continues on his path, calmly walking forward as if he doesn't notice the train as it passes just before he walks into it, his coat blows in the wind as it rushes by. The bright lights and tall buildings of the inner city loom in the distance, dwarfed by the massive cables of the space elevator that lie further beyond and ascend above the clouds. The tallest of all the buildings, the headquarters of the corrupt Takeshi Corporation, further known as T. Corp., captures his attention as if an unknown force draws him to it.

Suddenly, as if anticipating the incoming danger, he does a back flip, dodging a spiked ball and chain as it misses him by mere centimeters, he drops his bag in the process. He grips his sword in hand, still sheathed, as he calmly awaits his attacker's next move. The attacker wastes no time, spinning his ball and chain in a flurry of attacks as he steps into the open; clearly frustrated by the fact that his attacks are not connecting as the

16

man in the coat swiftly dodges everything he throws at him.

Seizing his opportunity, the man in the coat performs an aerial cartwheel, unsheathing his sword as he cuts the chain swinging under him and sheathes his blade before his feet touch the ground. As the spike ball slams into a nearby wall of a building the attacker stands still in amazement, holding what's left of the chain as it dangles to the ground.

He is a tall, muscular man with dark skin and finely groomed dreadlocks tied back with a rubber band. They both stand still staring at one another.

"Damn man, you owe me a new chain," Brock says. "I almost had you that time."

"Not even close," Yori says.

"Ha ha Yori! How long's it been mate? You know you're gonna get your ass killed walkin' 'round here like that," Brock jokes as they grip each other by the forearm and pat each other on the back. "Good to see you mate, I was starting to think you weren't comin' back."

"Well here I am," Yori says.

"You know shit's been pretty rough since you been gone man," Brock says.

"Yeah?" Yori says.

"Corp's been crackin' down hard," Brock says as they walk off in the distance toward the inner city.

Where the wasteland meets the city's edge, soldiers gather to investigate a gruesome scene, a whole squad of soldiers lie dead on the ground. Emerging from the background the leader of the gathering soldiers walks into view; dressed in battle ready armor from head to toe, face cloaked with a high tech mask and wearing a reddish coat, exactly the same as the one Yori was wearing.

Amongst the dead bodies is another squad leader dressed the same as him, yet his coat is missing, except for the sleeve still wrapped around his severed arm laying on the ground. The agent stands still over the bodies moving only his head as he surveys the area and pieces together the previous events in his mind.

"Sir?" one soldier says as he arrives at his leaders side.

"Bag 'em and return to base," he responds after a moment

of silence. "The rest on my six."

They begin to follow clues that lead them further into the city, cautiously tracking the squads killer.

Back at T. Corp. Headquarters Professor Kenji Yamato sits in his office having an uneasy discussion with a shadowy figure via video-chat on his holographic display.

"So far everything seems excellent," Kenji explains. "There are no signs of mutation, vitals are normal. We'll run physical tests after the mental exam."

"You have two hours. I better have my results by then," the man sternly replies as he shuts off his feed.

Just then the girl who was being monitored enters the room.

"Oh, Miyu my dear! How are you this morning?" Kenji startlingly sputters.

"I'm fine Grandpa," Miyu replies. "I thought I heard voices in here, is everything alright?"

"Oh? Oh, yes! Yes my dear, everything is just fine. How

are you?" Kenji says as he glances around the room in a paranoid fashion.

"Uh, yeah. You already asked me that Grandpa," Miyu replies slightly concerned as she tries to figure out what Kenji is looking for.

"Oh, I did? Oh yes, yes. Apologies," he says.

"I had that dream again last night," she says hesitantly after a short moment of silence.

"That's two nights in a row," Kenji quickly replies as he looks over some charts.

"Yeah but this time was... different," Miyu softly says.

"What do you mean?" he replies with a puzzled look on his face.

"Well this time, I... I saw—" she continues with an uneasy look on her face.

"Yes? What did you see?" he interrupts. "Tell me what you saw Miyu."

"I... I saw some kind of monster... It was eating someone. Then it attacked me," she answers with a frightened look.

"Come my dear! Let's start your training," he says in a hurried state as they exit his office.

As they walk down the hallway Kenji starts to whisper unusual things to her, catching her by surprise.

"Miyu listen to me, this is extremely important. You are more capable than you know. Stronger, faster, smarter," he says. "These people, everything around you is not as it seems. Do you not sense it? They're all watching you, studying your every move, they're all around us... You must escape, trust no one. There is an emergency stairwell around the corner to the right, I'll cause a distraction for you. Run, run far away from this place and never return."

"Grandpa what are you talking about? I belong here, with you," she whispers back.

"Forget about me my dear, focus on the task at hand. Go, now!" he frantically replies as he pushes her through the stairwell door.

She regains her balance and glances through the glass on

the door in time to see everyone rushing toward her, Kenji trying to block some armed soldiers from getting to her.

"Run Miyu!" he cries out as they throw him to the ground and restrain him.

In a panic, not fully aware of the situation, she begins to flee down the stairs as they give chase. The soldiers burst through the door, first looking up the center of the shaft then down, noticing her below they open fire. Startled, she dives away from the railing desperately looking for a way out.

More soldiers enter the stairwell a few floors down. Not able to go up or down, her only option is through the door next to her. She frantically makes a run for it through the door, knocking down a few employees as she makes her way down the hall.

Soldiers burst through the door from the stairwell and open fire down the hallway, mowing down a few employees in the process, as Miyu leaps over and behind a counter at an intersection at the other end of the hall. As debris flies all around her from bullets tearing through her surroundings she notices a door to her left and quickly makes her way through it.

She runs through the next few rooms and is reunited with another part of the previous hallway that snakes around the rooms. She weighs her options quickly and decides to double back to the stairwell. The ensuing soldiers burst through the rooms and into the hallway as they fan out in search of the suspect.

Down the hall around a corner Miyu notices a few shadows along the wall with weapons coming toward her and she ducks into the room closest to her on her right. As the soldiers pass they stop to check the room, lazily opening the door, glancing around then going about their business, not noticing Miyu hiding just a few meters away.

A short moment later she cautiously exits the room, checking both ways for soldiers before advancing down the hall once again. She passes the bullet ravaged counter and bloody corpses of the unfortunate bystanders as she reaches the stairwell door. She opens the door only to feel a piercing pain, her face struck with fear and uncertainty.

Glancing down she sees a syringe sticking out of her chest, the contents of which are already rapidly coursing through her veins. Everything around her suddenly slows and becomes hazy as she looks up at the man holding the syringe, the very same man who was watching her from behind the glass. The sedatives take hold and she falls to the floor as the cloudy outline of the man fades into darkness.

CHAPTER III.

THE GREAT ESCAPE.

*H*ot on the trail of their suspect, the group of soldiers tracking the elusive killer stumble upon the scene where Yori and Brock met just a short while ago. Their leader, same as before, stands still observing the area for a moment while the rest of the soldiers spread out searching for clues.

He calmly walks over to the spiked ball still stuck into the wall, with one hand he lifts the chain and observes the cut link. He walks away from the wall, kneels and observes the ground slowly scanning the area.

"There was a confrontation here," he says. "Two suspects, interesting."

"What is it sir?" one of the soldiers says.

"Neither is injured," he says. "Look there."

They notice a pair of footprints in some mud next to a puddle walking side by side.

"What does it mean?" the soldier responds.

"They left together," he says. "They must know each other."

He kneels down and touches the mud then rubs his fingers together.

"We're close. Stay sharp," he says following in the direction of the footprints as the sun sets in the west.

"Miyu," a muffled voice calls out from the darkness. "Miyu... This is extremely important. Listen to me," the voice continues as it echoes through the void.

She begins to see foggy visions of the past few days of her life, not knowing if it was all just a dream.

"You are more capable than you know... Stronger, faster, smarter... You must escape... Trust no one. Focus on the task at hand," the voice continues becoming more clear. Suddenly, as if she were back in the stairwell looking through the glass, she clearly hears her grandfather yell, "Run Miyu!"

She is instantly startled awake, more alert than ever, breathing heavily as she finds herself locked in a dark barren room practically naked, hanging in the center by chains shackled to her wrists. She looks around the room and hears a few guards just outside the door. Trying not to draw attention to herself she begins to try and free herself as quietly as possible.

On the edge of the inner city Yori and Brock are at a pub reminiscing.

"You've been gone a long time mate," Brock says.

"Yeah," Yori says.

"I'm surprised you lasted that long in the wastes," Brock says. "You find what you were lookin' for?"

"Not really," he replies. "I guess that's why I came back."

"That's it huh?" Brock says.

"Well that and I wanted to make sure Eli was taking care of you guys," he says. "It has been quite a while, I'm kind of nervous to see them again."

"Ah don't be mate," Brock says. "We all know why you left, it's just good to have you back."

"I'm not sure how long I'll be staying," he says.

"You know you're the first to kill one of those agents wearin' the coats," Brock says.

"The guy was an asshole," he says. "What's up with them anyway?"

"They showed up about a year ago," Brock explains. "Word is they're some sort of genetically altered freaks designed by the Corp. Another layer of security I guess, tryin' to snuff out the last little bit of freedom we have."

Outside the pub the group of soldiers emerge from the alley across the street. They come to a halt and observe the area as their leader yet again assesses the situation. Looking around the area he realizes that if they are still in the area the only logical place they would be is the pub. They make their way across the street and begin to surround the pub, preparing to flush the suspects out.

"Two around back. You two stay here, watch this exit. The rest on my six," their leader says as they begin to head inside the pub.

Brock notices the soldiers as they enter and begin conversing with the bouncers.

"We got trouble," he says as one of the bouncers points in their direction.

"How many?" Yori replies as his back is turned to them.

"Four. One's an agent," Brock answers as the soldiers walk in their direction.

Yori nods toward the rear exit then glances down at a pulse grenade he has tucked away in his hand.

"Oh shit," Brock says as his eyes widen. "You're one crazy motherfucker."

They head toward the rear exit casually, trying not to draw attention to themselves as the soldiers slowly make their way through the crowd. Just before they reach the rear exit the agent spots them and quickly pursues, violently pushing people out of his way. Yori drops the pulse grenade at the rear exit as he and Brock burst through the boor in full sprint, catching the two soldiers outside securing the exit off guard.

"Hey, freeze!" one of them shouts just as the pulse grenade detonates.

It releases a massive shock wave devastating its surroundings within a five meter radius and blows the soldiers back, injuring the agent still inside the building. The remaining soldiers hastily gather formation and give chase as frantic civilians scatter from the pub.

"They're after me not you, get outta here. I'll meet you at Betsy's," Yori says as they split up.

One of the guards outside Miyu's cell watches a live news feed on his holo-pad; a portable device worn on the forearm that projects holographic images and acts much like a smart phone.

"Hey check this out," he says to his colleague as the news broadcasts from outside the pub mere moments after the incident. "Wish I got some action like that instead of just standing around all the time," he continues as they watch the feed.

"You hear that?" the other guard says as he hears a faint noise coming from the cell.

"You're too paranoid man. Loosen up a bit," the other replies.

"Shh," he says after a moment of silence. "There!" he says as he hears a noise again.

The other guard turns off his holo-pad and slowly raises his weapon as they both move closer to the door, listening intently. Free from her shackles Miyu sprints from one side of the room to the other, leaping feet first into the door, blowing it off the hinges and onto the guard closest to the door. Catching the other guard by surprise she quickly disarms him and knocks him into the cell, rendering him unconscious in the process.

The man from behind the glass, the very same that injected Miyu with the syringe, has Kenji restrained in a room with several soldiers.

"After all I've done for you, this is how you repay me?" he says angrily.

Kenji, bloodied and bruised sits quietly in the chair with his head drooping.

"After all I've done for you—" Kenji begins to say before being struck by the man in charge.

Light peers into the room as the door cracks open and a soldier enters.

"Sir, we have a situation. S-cam 6," the soldier says frantically.

The man in charge brings up a live stream of the surveillance camera outside Miyu's cell on his holo-pad. Shortly after, Miyu makes her way out of the cell dressed in soldier garbs and picks up the soldiers weapon off the floor.

"Do not let her escape! I'll deal with you later," he says to Kenji as they quickly exit the room.

As Miyu hastily makes her way around the facility looking for a way out she travels down a hallway with one wall made entirely of windows and sees the real world on the other side for the first time. Realizing she is extremely high up in an enormous building she begins looking for a way down.

As she makes her way down a long empty hallway, soldiers come around the corner in front of her. She immediately opens fire as she strife's through a door and into the room on her left, hitting a few soldiers in the process as they frantically take cover and fire back. The soldiers gather themselves and strategically make their way to the door of the room.

As the first soldier enters Miyu kicks his weapon to the side with her left foot, followed by a right elbow to the face while she pulls a pin with her left hand from a grenade on his belt, then open palm punches his chest, knocking him into the others behind him as they all fly back into the hall against the wall on the other side.

She dives back further into the room as the grenade explodes, gouging a hole in the floors above and below with massive devastation. Knowing others are alerted to her location she wastes no time and jumps down the hole, making her way a few floors down just as more soldiers arrive amazed at the destruction. One of them looks down the hole and catches a glimpse of her as she runs out of sight.

"Suspect spotted on level eighty one," he calls over the com link.

Following the signs, she rounds a corner toward the stairwell and notices the elevator begin to open, filled with soldiers. She turns around and runs back around the corner as they exit the elevator and open fire, spraying debris everywhere as the bullets tear through the walls. They quickly give chase as she runs as fast as she can down the hall the way she came.

As she runs down the hall she stares out the wall made of windows at the end, seeing her freedom on the other side. Suddenly two soldiers come around a corner in front of her just as the rest following her make their way to the corner behind. The soldiers in front of her open fire and she drops to the ground sliding along the floor, bullets whiz overhead killing a few soldiers behind her as the rest duck behind the corner for cover.

She fires at the soldiers in front of her, one of them quickly dives away from harm the way he came. The other is frozen in fear as bullets fly all around him and fracture the glass behind, once the firing stops he frantically checks to see if he has been hit. Leaping out of her slide Miyu lunges into the air, planting both feet on his chest and grabbing him by the collar with one hand as they both fly through the window.

Only a few blocks away while running through the streets, Yori notices increased activity around the Corporation building and sees what appears to be several bodies jump through the window many stories above. He decides to investigate closer and heads down the alley toward the building.

Miyu rides the soldier down like an air board and punches him knocking him unconscious, then braces herself for a rough landing as they crash through the glass roof of a high class restaurant on top of the adjacent building and through a dining table below. Panic spreads in the restaurant as the guests frantically run for the exits. The soldiers gather by the window she leaped out of. Having no quick way to follow, the commanding officer requests a fly-in unit.

Immediately, as if anticipating the situation, a ship swoops in hovering along side the restaurant. Light from the ship peers through the windows as Miyu struggles to her feet out of the wreckage. A huge robot, a DX-39, leaps from the side door of the ship, it's weight causing the ship to sway. It bursts through the wall of the building clouding the room with dust and debris.

The DX-39 is a battle droid, it looks like an over sized

mechanical gorilla with no head, though it is not as quick or agile as a gorilla due to its massive weight. It has long, bulky arms equipped with fully automatic armor piercing guns and are littered with other numerous projectiles. It has larger missile pods around the shoulder area and has various sensors and cameras on its torso which allow it to see in many different spectrum's.

The robot scans the room quickly as the dust settles, acquiring its target. The hulking battle droid looms over Miyu and spins its torso around three hundred sixty degrees as it swings its arms at her. She ducks the first arm, not anticipating the second she is struck sending her hurtling across the room. She bounces off a pillar on the far side of the room breaking it in two. The pillar and part of the ceiling collapse as she wildly tumbles to the ground.

The robot sends bullets flying, punishing the surroundings as Miyu quickly rushes for cover and dives through a door into the kitchen area. As she goes through the emergency exit at the back of the kitchen the robot blows a hole in the wall with a small missile and begins to enter the room. She leaps from the scaffolding to the roof of the next building and makes her way down into the alley.

36

Still being followed by four soldiers, Yori enters an area between a few buildings and decides to set a trap for his pursuers. He makes his way to the rooftop of a small building and waits patiently for them to arrive. As Miyu makes her way down the alley she notices commotion ahead and hides, watching quietly in the shadows as the soldiers following Yori stumble into the area.

They creep in formation cautiously below him as Yori waits for his chance to strike. He waits patiently for the first two soldiers to pass, then as the last two are below him he leaps from the building in a sideways spinning motion. One of the soldiers looks up just in time to see Yori, sword unsheathed, coming down on top of him with such force he slices through his helmet and armor, splitting the soldier in two.

Guts spill to the ground along with both halves of the body as Yori quickly rolls to the next closest soldier. With a horizontal slice he cuts off the soldiers legs around the knees then sticks him to the ground through the chest with his sword. As the two soldiers leading the way turn around hearing the slaughter they receive throwing knives to their faces, dropping them instantly.

Yori removes the coat knowing it draws too much attention, he uses it to wipe the blood off his sword after removing the blade from the corpse, then tosses the coat aside. Sensing someone behind him he quickly turns around and notices Miyu coming out of the shadows. Having just seen him dispatch the soldiers and weakened from her ordeal she feels as if she has no choice but to trust him, despite what Kenji said.

Yori, standing still staring at this beautiful young girl wearing soldiers clothing that obviously isn't hers, looking as if she's been through hell, doesn't really know what to make of this strange situation.

"Please... Help me," Miyu says desperately as she slowly walks closer to him.

He glances over her shoulder in the direction she came from, noticing search lights from ships and soldiers combing the area for her.

"Come on," he softly replies as he holds out his hand.

She places her hand in his and they head off down the alley.

Shortly after they flee the area the injured agent from the pub stumbles upon the remains of his unit. He stands still observing the body parts, then walks closer to one of the bodies. He kneels down and pulls a throwing knife out of the soldier's face and looks closely at it. He realizes he is no match for the suspects alone and heads back to headquarters to report his findings and acquire backup.

CHAPTER IV.

INTO THE ORDINARY.

M*any* blocks away, deep in the outer area of the city, lies a dive bar named Betsy's Pub. Sitting at the bar, Brock is having a drink recalling the events that previously transpired to the bartender and owner, Marty Geiser. Marty is an older man, mid forties, shaved head; a business man and father, secretly working against the Corp. any chance he gets.

"Crazy bastard set off a pulse grenade inside the pub?" Marty says. "Ha, well there goes some of my competition."

"We had to split up after that," Brock says. "He told me he'd meet me here. That was like a few hours ago bro."

"You know Yori, fashionably late as always. He'll probably be comin' through that door any minute," Marty replies confidently.

Just then the door opens as Yori enters slowly, Miyu hiding behind him following closely.

"Speak o' the devil," Marty says.

"Damn, it's 'bout time bro! You had me worried," Brock says with a smile.

"Hey, Yori! Good to see you mate!" Marty says.

Elisa Geiser, Marty's spunky teenage daughter, comes running out of the back room as she overhears them welcoming Yori.

"Yori!" Eli says excitedly as she runs to him and gives him a hug.

"Sorry I'm late," Yori says calmly. "I brought a friend."

As he steps aside Miyu stands still, covered in dirt with an uncertain look on her face. After a moment of silence Elisa happily breaks the tension.

"Hi! I'm Elisa, you can call me Eli," she says. "That's Brock and my dad Marty over there. And this little girl is Chloe," she says picking her cat up off the counter, scratching her under the chin. "So, you got a name?" she continues as she puts Chloe down on the floor.

"Miyu," she quietly replies.

"Well it's a pleasure to meet you Miyu! You sure are a mess," Eli says as she touches Miyu's hair.

"Come on! Let's get you cleaned up," she continues as she takes Miyu by the hand.

As Miyu is pulled passed Yori she looks him in the eyes, they both smile while Eli continues to pull her to the back room.

"How on Earth did you get so filthy? And what's with the getup? You a cross dresser?" Eli says as she bombards Miyu with questions yet doesn't allow her time to answer. "You look about my size, I bet I got somethin' you can fit in. You don't talk much do you?" Eli rambles on as they head to her room.

"Shower's in here. I'll find you some clothes," she says as she starts going through her wardrobe.

"So, how long have you known Yori?" Eli continues as

Miyu begins to undress in the other room.

"Not long," she replies.

"He's awesome isn't he?" Eli asks.

Hesitating for a second Miyu replies "Yes," with a smile on her face.

"What's your favorite color?" Eli asks as she rummages through her clothes.

"I don't know," Miyu replies after some thought.

"What? How do you not know your own favorite color?" Eli quickly remarks. "You get bumped on the head or somethin'?"

"Maybe? I can't remember," Miyu says stepping into the shower.

"Well at least you remember your name!" Eli says optimistically. "Where are you from?" she continues.

"I'm not sure," Miyu replies.

"Not sure?" Eli says. "You don't even know where you were born?"

"Japan... I think," Miyu answers.

"Now we're getting somewhere. You have any relatives?" Eli asks still digging through clothes, tossing them all over the place.

As she recalls the past few days a few moments go buy, then Miyu replies in an uneasy tone, "My Grandfather."

"Aw, wish my grandpa was still alive. What's his name?" Eli asks.

"Kenji," she answers hesitantly.

"Well he sounds lovely," Eli continues. "I'd sure like to meet him. Kenji... That name sounds familiar. So, Miyu. You got a last name?"

"Yamato," Miyu answers without hesitation.

"Well, Miyu Yamato, definitely sounds Japanese. You sure you were born in Japan?" Eli continues.

"Yeah, I think so," she hesitantly replies.

"Well I only asked 'cause you look so young. Have you been in cryo-sleep or somethin'?" Eli asks.

"I don't think so, why would you ask that?" Miyu responds with a confused look on her face.

"'Cause Japan was wiped off the map like a hundred and seventy years ago, I thought everyone knew that. And you look so young, so you must have been in cryo-sleep or somethin'," Eli says. "You travel in space a lot?"

Miyu doesn't respond as she contemplates her recent findings. No matter how hard she tries, aside from her dreams of hazy childhood memories she only recalls the past few days.

"Well Miyu, I set some clothes out for you on the bed. I hope you like 'em. I'll be right outside if you need anything else," Eli says as she exits the room.

Marty kicks the remaining lushes out of the pub and locks the door, switching the sign to read '*Closed*'. He and Brock begin to play a game of pool. Stepping out of the shower and into the other room, Miyu looks at the clothes laid out for her on the bed.

As she gets dressed she notices Elisa's stuffed kitty doll that looks almost identical to the one she had in her room back at the corporation. She picks it up, hugging it closely against her chest, as thoughts of the past race through her mind.

"Knock knock! You alright in here?" Eli says as she enters the room startling Miyu. "Ah! You like Mr. Whiskers?" she asks.

"I used to have one just like it," Miyu responds as she smiles.

"Really? That thing's an antique you know," Eli says. "They don't make 'em like that anymore, I had a tough time finding it."

"Wow, you look good when you're clean! Love the outfit by the way," she says laughingly. "Come on!" She grabs Miyu by the hand again as they head back to the others in the bar.

Brock leans over the pool table lining up his shot, blunt ash falling to the felt as he concentrates more intently than ever. Elisa barges in messing up his concentration just as he shoots, sending the queue ball flying off the table.

"Da, da da daaa! Presenting the new and improved, Miyu Yamato!" she announces as she twirls with her hands in the air.

Miyu shyly steps in behind her with a nervous smile on her face. Swept away by her beauty Yori stares at her speechless, jaw drooping as his eyes light up.

"Wipe that drool off your chin bro," Brock quietly jokes as he taps Yori on the shoulder, freeing him from her trance.

"Well well well, look at you!" Marty smiles.

"Yeah, nice job Eli," Brock chimes in as they continue their game of pool.

As Miyu approaches Yori they stare in each others eyes with smiles on their faces. His heart pounds harder and harder inside his chest as she comes ever closer. He tries with all his might to spit out any words, anything at all, to no avail.

She stops in front of him and he finally mutters the only word he can get to come out of his mouth, "Hi."

Her smile becomes larger as she replies, "Hi."

"You look amazing," he manages to say as they all have a laugh.

Elisa quietly heads off to a back room, anxious to find out more about their guest. Marty kicks on the radio and brings Miyu a drink as they begin to play a few games of pool. This being Miyu's first time Yori shows her the ropes.

He explains it's a precise game, all about geometry and velocity, as she learns surprisingly fast becoming better than all of them in a very short amount of time.

"You sure you never played this before girl?" Brock asks as Miyu runs the table.

Miyu just smiles and shrugs.

"I think we got a hustler in the house, ha ha!" he continues.

Over several more drinks they play more pool and cards, laughing and having a great time while the music never stops. Miyu is beside herself, thankful to be with such wonderful people, having a normal experience in the not so normal life she can remember.

She absorbs it all like a dry sponge in a bucket of water; every second, every joke, every facial expression, every laugh, everything about her new friends as she has the best night of her life that she can remember.

Finally feeling comfortable enough, Miyu falls asleep, leaning on Yori after her extremely confusing and rough day. With Brock passed out and Marty drunk as a skunk practically falling out of his chair, head drooping to the table, Yori looks down at Miyu leaning against him.

He brushes his fingers through her hair, gently caressing his palm against her cheek, fingertips on the back of her neck as he gets up and lays her down on the cushioned bench. He gets a cover and gently lays it over her, cautious not to wake her, then props himself in a chair against a wall so everyone is in view. As she lay there asleep he can't help but stare at her beautiful face, the last thing he sees as he dozes off, carrying her into his dreams.

A few blocks away from the corporation building Kenji and the head of the corporation are preparing to board the space elevator. The elevator itself is a massive torus housed in a structure at the base of giant cables made from a light weight, super strong material derived from spider silk. The cables are secured deep inside the Earth and run all the way up into space where they are attached to an orbiting space station.

Kenji and the mysterious man walk toward the elevator, escorted by a team of soldiers as supplies are being loaded onto the elevator. The agent that was previously tracking Yori walks along side them discussing the situation with his boss.

"I can track them down," he says as he hands over the throwing knife. "I need multiple units for support."

"Take four units, and two DX-39's," his boss says as they step into the elevator. "Bring the girl back, dead or alive. Fail me and I will kill you myself."

"Understood," he says as he bows his head and the elevator doors close.

"Four units?" Kenji says as the elevator begins to ascend the cables. "You're mad."

"I'm testing her," the man says. "If your analysis is accurate she shouldn't have any trouble with them."

"You're expecting her to defeat them?" Kenji replies.

"Yes," he says.

"I thought you wanted her captured?" Kenji says.

"I will monitor my team and her ability to adapt to difficult situations. I want to see what she is capable of," he says. "In time she will come to me. After all, I have her dear grandfather by my side."

For the first night she can remember with no nightmares, Miyu sleeps in longer than usual. As she wakes from her dream she finds herself covered up, still laying on the bench. Slightly disturbing to her the pub is empty, except for Chloe curled up next to her. She quickly sits up and looks around the room.

Suddenly she takes a deep breath in, she closes her eyes trying to imagine what is creating the magnificent aroma that so intensely fills her nostrils. Chloe jumps down from the bench and runs down the hall in the back of the room. Miyu soon follows, slowly moving closer to the smells origin, sniffing it out along the way as it becomes more intense. She makes her way into the back rooms, still cautiously moving ever closer to the glorious aroma.

As she walks down the hall she hears the merry voices of her friends as they carry on typical conversation. She stops in the doorway and crosses her arms, then leans against the wall and observes them as she cracks a smile. She admires the way Elisa and her father joke around while making breakfast for everyone, the calm demeanor of Yori as he quietly eats his food and the overly loud boasting of Brock as he cracks remarks from time to time.

Soon Brock notices her standing in the doorway.

"Hey hey, look who finally woke up," he teases.

"Good morning Miyu!" Elisa shouts excitedly. "Just in time, your plate's just about ready!"

"You must've had a rough day yesterday," Marty says. "I've never seen anyone sleep so heavy."

Yori sits quietly, going about his business as if he knew she had been standing there all along, not saying a word as he shovels food into his mouth. She takes a seat next to him as Elisa sets a plate of food on the table in front of her.

She closes her eyes as she breathes in the aroma of the freshly cooked meal on her plate. As she takes her first bite Chloe rubs against her leg, purring as loud as a chainsaw.

"Well, what do you think?" Eli asks.

"It's wonderful," Miyu replies with a smile on her face.

"Best damn cooks on the planet!" Brock chimes in as he licks his plate clean.

Marty has a seat at the table across from Miyu as he begins to eat, Elisa shortly follows sitting next to him.

"The way you looked when you first arrived I would've assumed you'd been through hell and back," Marty says as he breaks the silence. "Strange thing is there were no visible wounds on ya."

Miyu reflects on the events of the previous night as she eats with a confused look on her face. She vaguely remembers her fresh wounds healing almost as fast as they were being inflicted.

"Eli tells me you were born in Japan, is that right?" Marty cautiously asks.

"Dad, stop interrogating her! You're always trying to make our guests feel uncomfortable," Elisa abruptly butts in. "Let's just have a nice breakfast, then we can discuss it, alright?"

"Alright, alright. Settle down," Marty replies.

Elisa nervously smiles at Miyu while chewing a fresh bite of food.

CHAPTER V.

PRESENT, PAST AND FUTURE.

After breakfast everyone gathers in a room down the hall to the left of the pub sealed with heavy duty doors. Scattered about the room are various contraptions created by Marty and Elisa, such as mechanical and tech gadgets amongst other things. In the back of the room sits two exo-suits they built themselves, fully armored and equipped with digital HUD's, mini guns, micro missiles and numerous other gadgets. Elisa sits at a computer console as Marty turns out the lights.

"Let's see what you got Eli," Marty says as she enables a holographic projection of her computer screen.

"Well no offense Miyu, but a few of your answers to my questions yesterday didn't make much sense," Elisa says. "I've been doing some research on the topic. I'm not trying to be nosy, I just want to help you remember."

"Thanks," Miyu says smiling.

"Well, let's just say it was much tougher than expected to find any information at all. And what little I did find raised even more questions," she says. "I ran a search on your grandfather's name. It took me quite a while to find anything, but I managed to find out that he worked for the Takeshi Corporation."

"That's not cool," Brock says.

"By '*worked*' do you mean he no longer works for them?" Marty says.

"Well, that's where it gets a little strange," she says. "Is this him in the pic Miyu?"

She brings up an old picture of Kenji receiving a plaque for his accomplishments in genetic research, shaking the hand of a former T. Corp. executive.

"Yes!" she says.

"Well this pic was taken in Japan over two hundred years ago," she says.

"What?!" Brock says confused.

Miyu stands quietly trying to make sense of what she just

heard.

"When was the last time you saw him Miyu?" Elisa says.

"Yesterday," she says hesitantly.

"Are you positive?" Yori asks.

"Yes," she replies.

"Well that's not all, it gets a little weirder," Elisa says. "It seems that Kenji did in fact have a granddaughter named Miyu. The problem is it says there was an accident at some lab Kenji was working at in Japan at the time."

"What kind of accident?" Marty asks.

Miyu has an uneasy look on her face as she relives the horrific events that took place in her dreams.

"I'm not quite sure," Eli says. "The trail kind of goes cold there. But I found this old newspaper clipping," she says as she brings up the image.

The article headline reads, '*Tragic Accident Takes Fourteen Lives*'.

"So some freak accident killed a bunch of T. Corp.

bastards, so what?" Brock says.

"Well, I read the article," she says hesitantly. "Apparently among the dead were thirteen scientists... and a little girl."

Silence envelops the room, everyone turns to Miyu with a look of shock on their faces as tears of sadness and confusion begin to run down her cheeks.

"I'm not sure what all this means," Miyu says as she breaks the silence.

"Me either," Marty says. "Can you remember anything?"

"I... I've had dreams," she says.

"What kind of dreams?" Elisa says.

She is reluctant to say at first, taking a look around at each of them. She looks at Yori last and gazes in his eyes, after a brief moment he nods to her letting her know it's alright to tell them.

"In my dreams I'm a child, in the place my grandfather used to work at," she begins. "I'm following this butterfly, the most beautiful butterfly I've ever seen. I chase it through the halls of this building, and then it becomes dark... scary. I go into some room that's all messed up, I see someone in the distance—"

They can tell that she seems frightened and uneasy just talking about the dream as she pauses mid sentence.

"Then what?" Brock says.

"Give her a minute," Marty says.

"It's alright Miyu," Yori says comfortingly.

"Well, I think it's Kenji, but when I call to him he comes at me," she says. "It's some sort of monster... eating someone."

"Is that it?" Brock says.

"Well, I wake up when it jumps at me," she says.

"It's alright," Yori says as she buries her head in his chest. "You're safe with us."

"Do you remember anything else?" Marty asks.

"Just the past few days," she says. "Kenji told me I was in an accident, he didn't really explain. He was doing some tests on me, said it was part of the recovery process."

"What kind of tests?" Elisa asks.

"Examinations, a little blood work, mostly mental tests. He said he wanted to help me become healthy again," she says. "But yesterday he was acting a little unusual."

"What do you mean '*unusual*'?" Marty asks.

"Well he seemed out of focus," she says. "I think he was trying to tell me something but he couldn't say exactly, he seemed rushed. He said I was being watched by everyone that was around us. He tried to help me escape, but I'm not sure what I'm running from."

"What happened?" Elisa asks.

"People began to chase me," she says. "They got him, he tried to help me."

"Then what?" Brock says.

"It's alright," Elisa says seeing she is trying to remember. "Take your time."

"I ran," she says. "I should have helped him, it all happened so fast. They started shooting at me, and I just ran."

"I'm sure there wasn't much you could do," Elisa says. "Anyone in that situation would have done the same thing."

"There was a man—" Miyu continues.

"A man?" Marty says.

"I'm not sure who it was," she says. "He injected me with something. I've felt his presence before, but I'm not sure why, after that I blacked out."

"Is that it? How'd you end up here?" Brock asks.

"When I woke up, something changed... in me," she says. "I'm not sure what, but I felt good, confident, powerful. It's strange, but I managed to do things I never dreamed I could do. I can't explain it, but I just ran and managed to get away. I was about to give up, that's when I saw Yori. I'm not sure what it was, but I felt I could trust him."

Yori smiles at Miyu and she smiles back.

"I brought her here," he says. "They were chasing her, and me too. I couldn't just leave her there."

"You did the right thing Yori," Elisa says. "We'll figure this whole mess out."

"So, you died? And your grandpa's some three hundred something year old dude?" Brock says. "Am I the only one that doesn't know what the fuck's going on?"

"Can I ask a question?" Miyu says.

"Sure," Marty says.

"What exactly happened to Japan?" she says.

"Well, they say Mount Fuji exploded," Marty says. "And that, along with the rising sea levels sealed its fate under the waves."

"It's all a conspiracy," Elisa says. "No one really knows what happened for sure, volcanoes erupt, they don't explode. Well not that bad anyway, and there have been reports over the years of radiation in the area. My guess is some kind of nuke."

"Either way I bet those T. Corp. bastards had something to do with it," Brock says.

"They did manage to transfer the majority of their operation here, amongst other places," Marty says. "Let's get back on track."

"My grandfather," Miyu says. "He's in trouble, I have to help him."

"Right," Elisa says. "I managed to hack into pretty much every camera in existence. I'm running a trace on Kenji's face, hopefully it comes back with a match. Then we'll know where he is, just give it a few minutes."

"So, are you some sort of experiment?" Brock says. "Like those monsters you were talking about?"

Marty smacks him upside the head.

"What?" he says as Marty rolls his eyes. "I'm still confused."

"I don't know what I am," she says.

"I do," Yori says softly. "You're alive, a living breathing human being, just like us. You have feelings, emotions, family... friends."

Through her disturbing thoughts his kind words bring a smile to her face.

"I'll do everything I can to help you get your grandfather back," he says as he wipes a tear from her cheek.

"Thank you," she says.

"Bingo!" Elisa says.

Her trace finds a match for Kenji and shows the live feed from the camera on her display. He is in a room with a man that has his back turned to the camera, surrounded by guards.

"That's him!" Miyu says.

"Who's that guy?" Brock says.

Elisa freezes the camera feed as the man turns around to walk out of the room.

"Vincent," Yori says.

"That's the man that injected me," Miyu says. "You know him?"

"Unfortunately," Marty says.

"Who is he?" Miyu asks.

"He's head of T. Corp." Marty says. "Been givin' us shit for years."

"Eli, where is this?" Yori says looking at the feed.

"Well, you're not gonna like it," she says. "It's on T. Corp.'s space station."

"Then that's where we're going," Yori replies.

"You're crazy man," Marty says. "You can't just walk on that elevator, and even if you did manage to get on that station it's filled with lackeys. It's suicide!"

"Just call in some favors and get me on that station," he says. "I'll worry about the rest."

"I'll see what I can do," Marty says as he steps out of the room to make some calls. "I can't make any promises."

Miyu slowly walks over to the wall, turning her back toward the others, lost in thought.

"You alright?" Yori says quietly as he approaches her, placing a hand on her shoulder.

"Yes," she says. "I'm going with you."

"It's gonna be dangerous," he says.

"I know," she says. "You don't have to worry about me, I can take care of myself."

"Alright," he agrees. "I trust you."

"Thank you," she says.

"Don't mention it," he says.

"Look," she says. "I can't ask you to do this, if something happens to you—"

"You don't have to ask," he says interrupting her. "That's what friends do, stick together and help each other out. It took me a long time to realize that, but it's why I came back here."

"You have great friends," she says looking into his eyes.

"We," he says. "We have great friends."

They turn to Marty as he reenters the room and hangs up with a friend.

"Well, good news... if you want to call it that," he says. "Sven said he's got a shipment he's gonna take to the moon later today. He said you can stowaway in a cargo container 'til you reach the dock."

"Well that doesn't really get us anywhere," Yori says. "We're not trying to go to the moon."

"Well, that's where it gets interesting," he says. "He's got a few hour layover for unloading, then he said on the way back he could '*swing by*' the station."

"That will have to work I guess," Yori says.

"Well, you know Sven," Marty says. "I'm not sure what he means by '*swing by*' but it probably ain't gonna be pretty."

"Yeah, but it's our only option," Yori says. "What do you think?"

"Ok," Miyu says as she nods.

"You know this is gonna bring a lot of heat," Marty says, Yori nods. "We should do somethin' 'bout T. Corps control over that damned elevator."

"Especially since they're probably making monsters up there," Elisa says. "We can't let them get away with something like that."

"What do you have in mind?" Yori says.

"Well, I'd like to get rid of it honestly," he says.

"I'm in," Brock says.

"Well, I think I have a pretty good plan," Marty says.

"Let's hear it," Yori says.

"The station has orbital thrusters that help keep the elevator and cables from dragging it back to Earth," he says. "If we can somehow unhook those cables down here—"

"It could pull the whole thing into space and send it out of orbit," Elisa says. "You might need to set the thrusters to full power to be able to lift that elevator out of orbit."

"How do we do that?" Yori says.

"Hold on a sec," she says as she pulls up a blue 3D schematic on her holographic display.

"Alright," Marty says. "This is a little complex, let's try to work out all the details."

They analyze the schematics and Elisa uses a blinking red light to pinpoint key locations as they discuss their plan.

"This is the control room here," she says as the 3D display pans and zooms to display the location on the upper most structure. "There are emergency escape pods here, here and here."

The display rotates and displays the pod locations, then zooms out to show the full structure with highlighted points of interest.

"We're still not sure how you're going to get on board," she says. "There should be signs that will lead you to where you need to go once you're in."

"No doubt that control room's gonna be guarded," Marty says.

"I can handle that," Yori says. "Once I'm in what do I need to do?"

"Well," Elisa says as she zooms into the control room allowing a more detailed view. "There's a panel here that should allow you to increase thruster intensity, beyond that I'm not sure."

"That control room's gotta have staff monitoring the systems," Marty says. "You could get one of them to help you with that."

"No problem," Yori says. "Can you bring up where Kenji is?"

"Sure," Elisa says. "I'll just trace where that camera is located and... there."

The display rotates and zooms to the location of a lab, tucked away in the middle of the structure, surrounded by corridors with strange structures along the walls.

"What's that?" Brock asks referring to the structures.

"Hard to tell," Elisa says.

"Looks like some sort of tubes," Marty says.

"If you can get to him you're gonna have to backtrack to the pods," Elisa says.

"Right," Miyu says.

"Alright, now what about us?" Brock says.

The display tracks the cables from the station to the base

structure on Earth as they observe the layout.

"The cables are anchored deep in the Earth," Elisa says. "But there's a weak point at the surface."

"Only problem is it's surrounded by an army," Brock says.

"Eli and I can take the exo-suits and cause a distraction," Marty says. "That should buy you enough time to slip in unnoticed."

"What kind of '*distraction*'?" Brock asks.

"Well, looking at this layout," Marty says. "I think our best option is for you to get into position here."

The schematic shows the massive structure, there are a few blocks of open terrain from the entrance to the adjacent buildings to the east. Marty is pointing out a tree line along the southern edge of the structure that Brock can sneak up to and use for cover.

"Eli and I will position ourselves in these buildings here and here," he says pointing to a building across the open terrain from the entrance and one on the edge of the northern block. "We can use the buildings for cover. We'll strike from here and that should draw them out from the entrance toward us. That should give you enough time to sneak in, and we should be able to hold them off there for a while."

"Alright, then what?" Brock says.

"Make your way here," he says as the display zooms in.

"Once you're inside it looks like there's a maintenance shaft here that will take you right to the cables," Elisa says.

"When you get there just plant these bombs on the cables," Marty says as he puts a pack of explosives on the table. "That should damage 'em enough to do the trick. You need to haul ass outta there after you set the charges though, no lollygaggin'."

"Yeah, we can't hold them off forever," Elisa says. "After you're in I'd estimate you have about five minutes to get the hell out."

"Get in and blow shit up! Sounds like my kinda plan!" Brock says, almost too enthusiastically.

"Those are some heavy duty explosives," Marty says. "You better make sure you get out in time."

"No problem!" Brock says.

"We need to time this perfectly," Elisa says. "Yori, you

and Miyu take these trackers. That way we can see when you're in position."

"Good call," Marty says. "Let's pack up and get to the shop. Yori, you guys need to get to the spaceport as soon as you can. Sven will be waitin' in bay twelve, but he ain't gonna wait all day."

"Thank you," Miyu says to everyone.

CHAPTER VI.

A TRIP TO HEAVEN.

J_{ust} outside across the street, a group of soldiers gather as a few units make their way to the back of the pub. Their leader, the same agent from the night before, stands still and switches his visor to a thermal vision mode as he scans through the walls for heat signatures.

"Squad in position, ready on your command sir," a soldier says as his team surrounds the building.

"Something's wrong," Miyu says as an uneasy feeling comes over her.

"What is it?" Yori asks.

She stands in silence, bracing herself against the wall with one hand, lost in a trance as she sees the danger closing in through what seems to be an out of body experience.

"We have to get out of here," she says coming out of her trance and turning to Yori. "Now!"

They head down the hall toward the pub trying to reach the rear exit. Just as they reach the pub flash bangs and smoke grenades come crashing through the windows as the front door is kicked in.

Soldiers come flooding through the door and open fire as Yori and Miyu run across the room and dive behind the bar. Debris flies through the air as bullets rip through their surroundings. As Miyu sits with her back against the bar covering her head, the sounds of gunfire and the sense of fear remind her of when she was in the same situation behind the counter at the corporation headquarters.

Yet this time something is different, she has Yori by her side; friends fighting for her, stopping at nothing to protect her and make things right. Slowly her fears begin to melt away. Suddenly Brock comes in from the side hall and opens fire with a fully automatic gun almost as big as he is, mowing down a few soldiers and turning the tides in their favor.

"Stay down!" Yori says as he chucks a pulse grenade over the bar toward the door.

He stands up and fires a few rounds from his handgun, taking out a few soldiers before grabbing Miyu by the wrist. They both run toward the rear hall as the pulse grenade explodes. The shock wave violently hurls them into the hall as it demolishes the front of the building. After the blast Brock quickly makes his way to the rear hallway. Marty and Elisa follow shortly behind, wearing the exo-suits.

As the dust settles a DX-39 robot smashes through the scattered rubble and blindly fires toward the rear of the building. Huge bullets tear through the building around them as they frantically race down the hall toward the back room and dive to the floor. The robot advances through the rubble and the leader of the soldiers enters behind. While on her stomach covering her head, amongst the confusion, Miyu looks to her left and notices Chloe frozen in fear.

When the firing stops they seize the opportunity and run for the back door. Once at the rear exit Yori turns around and notices that Miyu isn't right behind him. Just before he goes back to find her she exits through the dust in the hall carrying Chloe in her arms.

Just outside the back door several soldiers lay in wait, ready to ambush the fleeing fugitives. They hear the commotion coming from inside and they anxiously await the inevitable with guns drawn pointing at the door. The door bursts apart, pieces flying everywhere. Marty and Elisa emerge donning their exo-suits, ready for battle.

The soldiers open fire but their bullets have no effect against the superior armor of the suits. Elisa leaps into the air toward the group on the right and lands on the closest soldier, smashing him into the ground as she opens fire with her mini guns on the surrounding soldiers. Marty launches two micro missiles at the group on the left, hitting two in the chest blowing their flesh to pieces.

The suits are extremely quick and agile with devastating fire power. Yori, Miyu and Brock emerge from the door in time to see the carnage.

"Damn, those things are awesome!" Brock says as he

slings his big gun over his shoulder.

"Come on, this way!" Marty says as he and Eli hop down the alley with the rest following closely behind. "We gotta get to the shop."

As they round the corner at the end of the alley the DX-39 robot bursts through the back of the building and into the alley, shortly followed by the agent and what's left of his squad. He quickly assesses the situation.

"That way!" he says and they quickly give chase.

"Thanks for redecorating the pub back there Yori," Marty says.

"Don't mention it," he replies.

"I let Sven know you're comin'," Marty says as they continue to flee. "His shipment departs in a few hours, you gotta get to the damn spaceport fast."

"Yo, we got company!" Brock yells from the rear.

"These bastards don't know when to quit," Marty says. "Eli, get to the goddamn shop and fire up ol' Betsy. I'll hold off these sons of bitches!"

"I'm not leaving you here!" Eli replies.

"I'll be right behind ya dammit, get yer ass in gear!" Marty says.

"Don't worry Eli, I got his back," Brock says.

She nods to Brock and reluctantly obeys his orders. Miyu hands Chloe to her.

"Thanks Miyu," she says, grateful that Miyu saved her cat.

"Don't mention it," Miyu replies with a smile on her face.

She smiles back before quickly fleeing the scene. Marty and Brock setup an ambush for the quickly approaching DX-39 and company while Yori and Miyu head to the spaceport and Elisa heads to the shop.

The soldiers advance down the streets of the slums, unaware of the inevitable situation about to occur. As they step in range Brock opens fire from behind cover with his massive gun, hitting several soldiers as the rest panic and scatter like roaches hiding from the light. The agent takes cover behind the DX-39 robot, using its armor as a shield. The robot locks on to Brock's location in an abandoned store front ahead on the left side of the street and its missile bay doors suddenly open.

"Oh shit!" Brock says.

He quickly runs further into the shop, trying to reach cover as the missiles tear through the air toward the store. He is hurled through the air toward the stock room in the rear as the missiles explode causing massive damage to the structure, burying him in rubble.

The agent exits cover from behind the robot and advances toward what's left of the store front as the dust settles. Only a few meters away from the store, he suddenly notices six smoke trails, flying in formation, rise up from a rooftop to the right. He watches them closely as they arc thirty meters in the air and begin to descend on the robots location.

Realizing what is about to happen, he has no time to react as they come crashing down on top of the robot, exploding with such force they practically level the whole block. The shock waves from the blast send the agent flying diagonally through the front corner of the store and into an alley on the other side.

The smoke clears and surprisingly, although heavily damaged, the DX-39 is still intact. As it regains its bearings Marty leaps from the roof tops, extends a giant blade on the arm of his suit and lands on top of it, plunging the blade through its weakened armor, deep into its circuitry. While losing hydraulic fluid and struggling to stay balanced, it spins its upper torso around tossing Marty aside.

He bounces off the wall of a nearby building and hits the ground. The robot immediately opens fire with its mini guns, but the agility of his suit allows Marty to hop around with such speed that he avoids being struck by the bullets as they trail closely behind him. The commotion caused by the recent explosions has alerted nearby Corp. fly-in units known as Talons and they begin closing in on the location.

The agent struggles to his feet in the dusty alley way, shaken from the impact. Before he is fully erect Brock jumps out from the demolished store and punches him in the side of the head with all his body weight behind the blow. He quickly follows with an uppercut from his other fist, knocking the soldier back as parts of his mask shatter and fly through the air.

He anticipates Brock's next move, catching the incoming fist with his hand, then punches him in the chest. The strength of the blow sends Brock flying back into the wall. The agent slowly advances as Brock staggers to his feet.

"You worthless being, do you think you can defeat me?" he says. "I will find your friends and rip their hearts out with my bare hands."

"Fuck you asshole," Brock replies as he spits blood on the ground.

"Such childish words. I expected more from you," he says. "Enough playing, time for you to die."

He grabs Brock by the throat and lifts him off the ground with one arm. As Brock struggles to breath he raises his arms above his head and locks his hands together. He brings them down on the agents elbow with all his might, freeing him from his grasp.

His feet hit the ground and he quickly head-butts the agent, effectively stunning him, then leaps in the air and knees him in the face. He tackles the agent while he's off balance and begins to smash his head into the ground repeatedly with his forearms as he sits on top of him. The agent knees him in the back, then throws him off in the direction of the street.

Across the street Marty takes refuge from the wounded DX-39 deep inside the narrow confines of a building. The robot fires a few missiles at the building, gouging a big enough space for it to advance. It traverses through the dust and rubble, deeper into the building in search of its prey.

From the darkness of a long hallway extending toward the back of the building, two missiles fly straight at it. With no room or time to maneuver the missiles nail their target, causing more damage to the hulking machine. Before it has time to recover Marty leaps from the hallway, lands directly in front of it and uppercuts through its torso. The robot drops to the floor like a bag of bricks as the long blade rips through its machinery.

Brock takes a few more swings at the agent to no avail. The agent blocks each of his attacks with the same arm then punches him with his free hand. The powerful punch sends Brock flying into the street. As the agent slowly walks toward him, Brock sees part of his face through his broken mask.

"You're one ugly motherfucker," he says lying in the street.

"Small price to pay for such power," he replies as he moves ever closer. "Any last words?"

"Eat this!" Marty shouts from across the street.

The agent turns his head just in time to see a micro missile slam into his face then explode. It blows most of his torso into bits and his legs fall to the ground.

"I don't think we'll be seein' him again anytime soon," Marty says as he helps Brock to his feet.

The Talons come hovering over the roof tops looking down on the devastation, their guns take aim at Marty and Brock.

"Get down on the ground," a voice calls out through the speakers.

"Now what?" Brock says.

"You have three seconds to comply," the voice continues.

Two seconds later the guns begin to spin, preparing to fire as Marty and Brock await their inevitable doom. Suddenly, as if out of nowhere, the Talons are struck by several missiles.

As they crash to the ground Elisa flies overhead in Marty's modified ship and touches down in the street. The rear bay doors of the ship open and Elisa comes out to greet them as they climb aboard.

"Goddamn am I glad to see you girl!" Marty says. "You sure know how to make an entrance."

"There it is," Yori says as he and Miyu reach the outer wall of the space port. "We need to find a way over."

The wall stands before them, eight meters high with guard towers every hundred meters.

"Grab the top," Miyu says. "I'll give you a boost."

"What?" Yori says.

"Trust me," she replies as she holds out her hands.

He puts his foot in her hands and she gently tosses him to the top of the wall. He quickly jumps down the other side and waits for her. She takes a few steps back then jumps toward the wall, with one step midway up she propels herself up and over.

"You're amazing," he says quietly, making her blush.

At the cargo transport Sven checks the time and looks around in a paranoid manner, smoking a cigarette while his crew finishes loading the shipment. Yori and Miyu step out from behind one of the crates and approach him.

"Yori!" he says relieved as they shake hands. "Been a long time mate. I didn't think you were gonna make it."

"How ya been Sven," he says as they board the ship.

"Hangin' in there, no thanks to the Corp." he replies. "Marty said you were bringin' a friend." he says as he looks Miyu up and down.

"Something wrong?" Yori asks.

"Nah, I just wasn't expecting... well, her," he says. "What's a beautiful young lady such as yourself hangin' around with this guy for eh?"

Miyu stands there silently, not knowing how to answer the question.

"Ah, doesn't matter. You guys hang out here with the cargo and put these on," he says as he hands them some uniforms. "When we get there just act like you're part of the crew. Leave your weapons here in the cargo hold."

The long, curved magnetic launch rails of the space port glisten in the sun as the cargo transport takes off on rail three. On board the space station Kenji is forced to continue his experiments. His current subject, Vincent, is strapped to a table awaiting the new breakthrough treatment in cellular regrowth.

Surrounded by guards watching his every move Kenji has no choice but to obey Vincent's every command, helping him become an unstoppable abomination. He stalls as long as he can, moving slowly and nervously looking around the room.

"It's inevitable," Vincent says. "It's been this way for hundreds of years, you don't have a choice in the matter. It is your destiny to make me a god."

Kenji lowers his head in shame as he sticks the syringe into Vincent, injecting its contents into his veins. Vincent laughs maniacally as the fluids course through his body.

The moon progresses in its orbit, rich with traffic coming and going, bright lights of colonies scattered about its surface and satellites orbiting over head. Sven's cargo transport sits freshly docked in sector seven, his crew working tirelessly to unload its shipment.

Stepping out from the cargo hold, Miyu is speechless as she gazes upon her new environment. Looking up at the see-through ceiling, past all the transport vessels flying overhead, she sees Earth in the distance, partially lit up by the sun.

"It's beautiful," she says.

Yori takes her by the hand, she turns to him and smiles.

"Come on," he says as they head toward the entrance to sector seven's market district.

As they approach the security checkpoint at the entrance Sven comes through from the other side.

"Hey there you guys are. I got you a room," he says as he hands Yori a room key. "Be back here in ten hours, we'll be ready to go."

Yori nods and they walk through the scanners into sector seven.

"Can we trust him?" Miyu asks as they walk through the crowd of people.

"Sven? Yeah he's an old friend of Marty and my father," Yori says. "I've known him since I was a kid, he's like family."

"He seems nervous about something," she says.

"Yeah he's like that," he replies as they make their way to the hotel.

Later at the hotel while Miyu is in the shower, Yori removes his shirt and sits on the corner of the bed by the window.

He looks down at a picture in his hand taken by an antique Polaroid, colorful glowing signs outside illuminate the otherwise dark room. Miyu comes out from the bathroom behind him, naked, her flesh still moist from the steam.

She sits on the bed behind him and notices the numerous scars on his bare torso. She gently touches them, slowly following them with her fingertips up his back. She wraps her arms around him and rests her chin on his shoulder.

"Who's that?" she asks looking at the picture.

"My father," he replies.

"What happened to him?" she says after a brief moment of silence.

"Killed by the Corp." he says. "I was six... I should have done more to help him... I saw the whole thing... I just hid. I'll never forget that face... The man that killed him."

"Who?" she asks.

"Vincent," he replies.

"I'm sorry," she says.

"Don't be," he says. "Marty and my father were like brothers. Marty raised me after that, Eli's like a sister to me. I'd do anything for them."

"What happened to your mother?" she asks.

"Died giving birth," he says.

"Did you really mean what you said back there?" she says. "That I'm not a monster. I'm, '*human*'... Like you."

He turns toward her and gazes into her eyes as she gazes back. He doesn't have to answer her question with words, she can see it in his eyes, feel it in his mind. They kiss, slowly at first, then more passionate. As she lies back on the bed she grabs his bulging, muscular arms and pulls him on top of her.

No more can he resist the electrifying love for her he has felt since the very first moment they met. It becomes more passionate and intense as they kiss and caress, holding each other tightly. He kisses her neck as she breathes heavily in his ear and inadvertently claws his back.

CHAPTER VII.

TWISTED REALITY.

Hours later back at the cargo bay Sven stands just as before, smoking a cigarette, awaiting the arrival of Yori and Miyu. They come walking up right on time, hand in hand.

"Not like you to be on time Yori," he says. "You guys enjoy yourselves?"

They look at each other and smile as they enter the ship.

"Marty let me in on your little plan, crazy as usual," Sven says. "Here's the deal, I can't dock with the station. We'd all be in deep shit before we even got close. I'll get as close as I can without their defenses shootin' us down, but you're gonna have to jump for it."

"Jump?" Miyu says.

"It's risky. There's a lot of factors involved here," he says. "The speed of my ship, the stations orbit, your rate of speed and angle of approach. I'll slow down as much as I can, but you gotta time it just right or you're a goner. I got a few suits for you, that's the best I can do... Listen, if you wanna back out I won't hold it against you, I can just take you back to Earth—"

"We're doing this," Yori interrupts.

"Alright," Sven says reluctantly. "Can't say I didn't warn you."

Sven's ship approaches the space station, kicks on the reverse thrusters and slows its speed. The bay door on the side of the ship opens slowly as Yori and Miyu get a glimpse of the approaching station in the distance.

"It's now or never," Sven says over the com. "Good luck."

Yori leaps from the ship toward the station holding Miyu's hand, his sword in the other. They have crossed the threshold into the vacuum of space, the point of no return. Sven watches them float helplessly toward the station from the cockpit as he approaches Earth.

Back on the Earth's surface Marty, Eli and Brock prepare for their assault on the elevator.

"The package has been delivered," Sven says over the com.

"No turning back now," Marty says. "You ready Brock?"

"I ain't gettin' any younger," he replies over the com.

Yori vents small bursts of oxygen out of the pack on his back strategically to compensate for their miscalculations and puts them on a proper course. Although heading straight for the station, as they get closer he realizes they are coming in too fast and tries to brace for a rough impact. They slam violently into the station at an angle, their momentum sends them tumbling out of control.

Miyu manages to grab hold of part of the structure just before they are ejected toward the atmosphere, still holding Yori's hand as he dangles into the void, looking at the Earth below. She pulls him to her, allowing him to get a grip on the station and they make their way to a maintenance hatch roughly ten meters away.

"Sir, one of the maintenance hatches is reporting a malfunction," a systems officer says.

"Let's see it," Vincent says and the officer brings up a view of the cameras in the vicinity on his display.

"Pressure is stable," the officer says as they observe the outside of the hatch, then switch to an inside camera.

They notice Yori and Miyu making their way down the hall adjacent to the hatch pressure room.

"Don't sound the alarm," Vincent says. "Send two squads to the labs."

Yori and Miyu sneak unseen further into the station, unaware they are being monitored, until they reach the escape pods.

"Follow the signs to the labs. When you find Kenji get back here," Yori says. "Get out in one of these whether I'm here or not."

"I'm not leaving you," she says.

"Don't worry, if I'm not here I'll be right behind you. Take this," he says handing her his gun. "And be careful."

"You too," she says after she kisses him.

He smiles and nods his head before running off in the direction of the control room.

Brock moves into position at the tree line just south of the elevator entrance, awaiting his opportunity to enter the structure. Scattered around are numerous guards and patrol personnel as well as two DX-39 robots guarding the front entrance.

Marty launches several missiles from a rooftop of an adjacent building, effectively taking out a handful of guards. The rest of them panic and try to find cover as they return fire.

"We're under attack!" a soldier shouts over the com.

Flanking them from a building to the north, Elisa has a clear shot at a group taking cover behind a defense wall. From her vantage point in the building she sends a few missiles out a window toward them, annihilating the group.

The soldiers regroup and advance on their locations in two separate groups, each taking one of the DX-39's with them. When they get far enough away Brock seizes the opportunity and makes his way inside, taking out a few remaining guards along the way.

Miyu sneaks past a few personnel and finally reaches the lab area on the station. Eerily empty, she slowly advances further through the dimly lit corridors. She looks on in horror as she passes monsters from her nightmares, hundreds, possibly thousands of grotesque mutations hooked to various machines in tube-like structures lining the walls. Chills roll down her spine as she cautiously traverses the corridors.

Yori spots the control room entrance just around a corner and at the other end of the hall. Heavily fortified and guarded by a few agents, he opts to find an alternate path of entry. He spots an air duct through a window in the room adjacent to him. A few personnel emerge from the control room, briefly averting the two agents attention.

Yori quickly makes his way to the room across the hall while they're distracted. He enters the air duct, crawls toward the control room, then stops at a vent. Looking through the vent below him he can see the various computer systems and personnel monitoring them, keeping the station properly aligned in orbit.

Kenji is locked in a room being observed and forced to continue his work with two soldiers guarding both sides of the door. Suddenly, he is startled by gun fire coming from outside the room. The soldiers inside with him hear the commotion as well, followed by silence. They decide to check out the situation and open the door to find the guards outside lying dead on the floor.

They cautiously emerge from the room in formation, nervously scanning the surroundings with their weapons while Kenji stands still in the room watching the door. After a few tense moments of silence, the sounds of a struggle and shots being fired startle him, then a soldier comes violently flying back into the room unconscious.

Miyu appears in the doorway shortly after the soldier hits the floor. Shocked to see her, Kenji doesn't know what to say as he slowly holds his arms out and takes a few steps toward her.

"Grandpa!" she says as she runs up and hugs him. "Come on, we have to go."

"How—" he begins to say, trying to get the words to come

out.

"No time, let's go," she says taking his hand.

They exit the room and run through the labs back toward the escape pods she passed on the way in.

Relatively unnoticed, Brock manages to place all the explosive charges in the strategic spots and primes them for detonation. Marty and Elisa are continuing to hold their ground outside, keeping the personnel unaware of the real threat. Marty emerges from out of cover and opens fire on the advancing units, then quickly leaps to safety as they return fire.

Elisa takes a more direct approach, leaping out at the soldiers as they try to surround her and kills several of them in close quarters. The rest of them fire frantically, trying to hit their target to no avail. They can't match the pace of Elisa and her exo-suit as she leaps around the environment. She continues to move too quickly for the DX-39 to lock onto her. It unleashes a torrent of lead at her as she runs diagonally along a wall then leaps to cover in an adjacent building.

On the space station Miyu and Kenji quickly run through

the monster filled corridors attempting to make their way out of the labs. As they round the corner they are greeted by a slew of soldiers flooding the lab entrance, blocking their escape.

The soldiers open fire down range without hesitation. Miyu turns, quickly tackling Kenji as they dive back around the corner. She abruptly returns fire using the corner as cover, killing several of them and wounding a few others.

"Miyu," Kenji says. "You have to get out of here."

She turns to him, shocked to see blood coming from his mouth as he lays on the floor propped against the wall. She begins to panic and looks him over with haste. She notices a tremendous amount of blood coming from a hole in his abdomen he is concealing under his hand.

"Leave me Miyu," he says in anguish.

"No," she says. "Hold on Grandpa."

"My time has passed," he says. "I'm sorry Miyu... for everything."

"Don't die on me," she says with tears flowing down her face.

"I'm not proud of the things I've done," he says. "But I am proud of you... I've lived a long life, a little too long. I'm tired, tired of being a prisoner, a slave. I'm just glad I could give you a second chance."

"You're gonna be alright, just hang on," she says as she fires a few more shots around the corner. "I'm gonna get you out of here."

One of her shots cracks one of the mutants containers, it awakes and quickly becomes aware of its surroundings. It smashes the rest of the way through the glass and attacks the nearby soldiers with furious rage as they scream in terror. Their bullets have little effect, the rest of the horrified soldiers run away in fear down the corridor on the right and the mutant gives chase.

"It's too late," Kenji says.

"Come on," she says lifting Kenji off the ground.

Seizing this unexpected opportunity, they head down the left corridor toward the escape pods.

Waiting for the right moment, Yori quietly jumps down from the air duct into the control room and lands behind the officer sitting at the control monitors. He quickly kills the two guards by the door with a pair of throwing knives then unsheathes his sword and places it on the officers throat close enough to cut his whiskers. The commotion of the fallen soldiers alerts the other officers in the room and they turn toward Yori. Realizing the severity of the situation, yet unsure what to do, they stand still in fear.

"Set the orbital ascension thrusters to one hundred percent," Yori commands the officer attached to his blade.

Fearing for his life, the officer hesitates and Yori tightens his hold, cutting him slightly. As a small amount of blood trickles down his neck the officer hastily complies. Before he can finish his given task however, a gun shot rings out echoing in the room. The officer is struck in the head, killing him instantly. On the far end of the room, holding the gun as the barrel smokes, is Vincent.

"Incompetence," he says as Yori releases the bloody corpse. "You must be the one that's given me so many problems over the years. How nice to finally meet you."

The other officers are petrified after seeing their colleague murdered in front of them by their employer. Yori glances over at them as they are frozen in place.

"You think I care about these pawns?" Vincent says, then suddenly shoots them as well. "Where is she?"

"Why would I tell you?" Yori says.

"She *is* on this station," Vincent says. "Tell me and I may let you live. Then again, I may not. Either way I will find her."

"What do you want with her?" Yori asks.

"That's none of your concern," he says. "I simply wish to have my property returned to me, to use as I see fit."

"She's not your '*property*'," Yori says.

"Ah, you couldn't be more wrong," Vincent explains. "You see, my company created her, and I am in fact the owner of said company. By law she is the property of my company, therefore I own her."

"You can't '*own*' a human being," Yori says.

"But she is not a '*human being*' as you put it," Vincent says slowly moving closer to Yori. "She is merely intellectual property, a product of my company's experiments."

"Which are illegal by the way," Yori says.

"These '*laws*' of which you speak do not pertain to this particular situation," Vincent says.

"That's far enough," Yori says raising his sword at Vincent. "She *is* human, and you can't have her."

"Who's going to stop me, You?" Vincent says. "And what exactly are you planning to do with that? I don't think you realize who you're dealing with boy."

Vincent tosses his gun to the side and strikes with such speed it catches Yori off guard. Yori bounces off of some equipment and hits the floor.

"I'm going to enjoy watching you die," Vincent says walking toward him.

He regains his footing and lunges at Vincent in a flurry of

precise strikes. As if predicting his movements, Vincent manages to dodge his blade. Yori ends the sequence of attacks with a backhand to Vincent's face and a spinning kick to his chest.

Not even knocked off balance, Vincent retaliates by punching Yori then grabbing and kneeing him before tossing him aside like a doll. Yori lands on the controls, tumbling through the equipment and off the other side.

He quickly regains himself, hiding behind the console he makes his way over to the side closest to the entrance of the room.

"It's been fun playing with you, but I'm getting bored with this game," Vincent says walking around the controls.

As he reaches the edge of the console Yori quickly jumps out, stabbing Vincent through the chest. As Vincent stands, run through by his blade, Yori slowly pushes it further into him. Vincent suddenly grabs Yori by the throat with his right hand, lifting his feet off the ground.

"Fair attempt, but you cannot kill me," Vincent says and grabs the blade with his left hand as the sharp edge digs into his

104

fingers.

With Yori still holding the hilt he slowly pulls it out.

"We'll see," Yori struggles to say, still suspended off the ground.

Unbeknownst to Vincent, Yori pulls a pulse grenade out with his free hand. Just as he activates it Vincent punches him in the chest causing him to drop the grenade at Vincent's feet and sends him across the room into the wall next to the door.

As Yori lay on the floor in certain defeat, Vincent gets a confused look on his face when Yori begins to laugh. Looking down he notices the grenade at his feet just before it explodes, crippling practically the entire control room. Yori rises to his feet with sword in hand and stumbles toward the door next to him.

On the other side of the door the two agents feel the explosion and turn toward the door in time to see Yori emerge and in one quick motion lob off their heads. Battered and bloody he staggers down the hall, making his way toward the escape pods as emergency lights flash and sirens begin to blare.

Carrying Kenji in her arms as she makes her way through the station, Miyu notices employees becoming frantic and rushing about as the emergency warnings begin. She takes it as a sign that Yori has accomplished his goal and will shortly be following her escape.

"We're almost there Grandpa," she says.

"I'm... so proud," he says as his eyes begin to roll into his head. "My child."

"Stay with me Grandpa," she says as they reach the escape pods.

Once inside one of the pods she collapses to the floor with him still in her arms.

"Hold on Grandpa," she says desperately. "Please don't die."

Holding his flaccid body, he is unresponsive and appears to be dead. She frantically tries to help him regain consciousness by holding his head up and repeatedly tapping him on the cheek.

"No... wake up," she says. "Grandpa? Please! Look at me,

come on."

He slowly takes a deep breath in, opening his eyes and focusing on her face as she hovers over him. Her tears drip down onto him, he reaches up and places a hand on her cheek.

"Don't cry my dear," he says with a smile as he takes his last breath.

His hand falls from her face and his neck muscles give way to the weight of his head as it droops down over her arm. She takes his hand and touches it against her cheek again, then releases it and it falls just as before.

She tightens her grip around him, hugging him close, burying her face into his shoulder and lets out the heavy cry she has been holding back. Soon after, she wearily stands up and hits the manual release of the escape pod, ejecting it toward the Earth's surface.

Back on the surface the battle wages on, Marty and Elisa are beginning to struggle a bit with the overwhelming bombardment from the corporation soldiers and droids. Pinned down and heavily outnumbered, all hope seems to be lost when suddenly the explosives detonate at the base of the elevator.

The blast tears the structure to pieces, sending chunks of rubble flying through the air. Shock waves devastate the surrounding area crumbling the buildings in the vicinity, some of which collapse under the stress and tumble to the ground.

Huge chunks of debris are hurtled through the air as tremors shake the the Earth. Clouds of dust fill the air and smoke from the blasts bellow from the carnage. Some of the soldiers surrounding Marty and Elisa are crushed by chunks of the buildings falling to the ground. Marty and Elisa use the cover of the thick dust and chaos of the falling rubble to slip away from the soldiers grasp.

They rendezvous with Brock a few blocks away where they have Betsy parked. The cables supporting the elevator whip around destroying anything in their path, gouging the Earth's surface as they drag about. The sheer weight of the cables with the elevator attached begins pulling the station into the Earth's atmosphere.

Inside the space station mass hysteria envelops the crew as it thrashes about. Being tossed back and forth, Yori slowly makes his way through the corridors. More systems seem to be failing every second in light of the current situation. Suddenly the artificial gravity goes out and Yori begins to float, weightlessly suspended above the floor.

He uses this to his advantage, propelling himself quickly through the station by pushing off walls while dodging various hazardous objects floating about. He soon reaches the escape pods and manages to eject from the station just before it breaches the atmosphere.

CHAPTER VIII.

HELL UNLEASHED.

The station violently enters the atmosphere, some parts are ripped loose while others burst into flame. In the control room Vincent struggles to the control console and manages to hit the emergency cable release, which effectively detaches the elevator cables from the station.

He then engages the orbital altitude thrusters to maximum, slowing the stations descent. Due to the weight and velocity in which it is currently traveling, the station's thrusters cannot overcome gravity as it falls to the surface. With a steadily decreasing rate of speed, there is simply not enough time to stop the inevitable.

After a rough landing Miyu is safely on the ground.

Standing just outside the pod she came down in she looks on in horror as the station falls from the sky and the cables come crashing down. She soon notices another escape pod fly overhead and crash down a few kilometers to the west of her location.

The cables, along with the elevator, violently crash to the surface, ripping through the environment, smashing anything in their path. They tear through buildings and splash through the lake, displacing enormous amounts of water, then crash down over the mountains and extend kilometers beyond.

Frantic civilians are terrified at the sight of the massive station looming overhead as it advances toward them and the devastation the cables have caused. Some are helpless to avoid disaster as waves of water rush through the lower section of the city with enough force to devastate the area before receding back into the lake.

The thrusters slow the stations descent enough to not be fully destroyed in the impact as it comes crashing down on top of the T. Corp. building and several surrounding blocks near the center of the city. People inside the building are unable to alter their demise as the building is ripped apart and crushed under the station.

The force of the impact leaves the station severely
mangled as its remains violently come to a halt. Smoke, dust and
debris are ejected kilometers across the terrain, blanketing the city
in an eerie fog. The entire city is massively devastated from the
tragic event.

In the wake of the impact riots break out, the scattered
remnants of corporation forces try desperately to secure each
sector as conflicts escalate across the city. Miyu stares at the
twisted wreckage of the space station in the distance, still
relatively intact. She glances down for a brief moment at Kenji's
corpse, still warm in her arms, then turns her attention to the
station again as tears trickle down her face.

Somehow deep inside her she knows Vincent survived the
crash, she can feel the energy of his life force coming from within
the station. Marty's ship approaches her location and hovers
overhead, then slowly descends as the rear bay doors open.

"You made it! We saw the pod come down just before the

explosion," Brock says as Miyu hands him Kenji's body.

He takes the body further into the ship as Elisa comes running back from the cockpit. She slows down for a second to glance at Kenji's body then continues to run to Miyu.

"Where's Yori?" she asks.

"Over there," Miyu says as she turns and points in the direction where the other pod came down. "Please, make sure he's alright."

"Wait," Elisa says as Miyu begins to advance toward the station. "Where are you going?"

Miyu doesn't respond as she makes her way into the distance.

"Miyu!" Elisa calls out in desperation.

Off in the distance, battered from the landing, sits the escape pod Yori came down in. The door is jammed shut due to the frame being bent but Yori manages to kick it open. Slightly bloody and bruised he slowly climbs out and falls to the ground. He looks around at the carnage that surrounds him, a city in shambles.

Marty's ship touches down close by and Brock and Elisa come running toward him followed shortly by Marty.

"You alright bro?" Brock says as Yori struggles to his feet.

"Yeah, not exactly what we had in mind," Yori says as he looks at the destruction around him.

"What the hell happened up there?" Marty says.

"I ran into a few complications," Yori says. "Where's Miyu?"

"She took off toward the station," Elisa replies.

"Kenji?" Yori says.

"He didn't make it," Brock says.

"Get the hell out of here before the Corp. shows up," Yori says as he gets his weapons and gear out of the pod.

"Where the hell you think you're goin'?" Marty says.

"To help Miyu," Yori says.

"We're coming too!" Elisa says.

"The hell you are. Get as far away from here as fast as you

can," Yori replies.

"And where would that be? My pub's destroyed, the shop's no place for a home and the damn Corp. bastards are crawlin' 'round everywhere," Marty says. "They're sure to be lookin' for us after that stunt."

"I hear Mars is nice this time of year," Yori says as he heads toward the station.

"Damned smart ass son of a bitch," Marty says.

"Yori! Wait," Elisa says as he walks off in the distance.

"Well, what now?" Brock says looking out over the city.

Miyu sneaks through the streets advancing ever closer toward the station, trying to avoid being spotted by the Corp. as they deal with the outraged civilians. The corporation network suddenly posts an A.P.B. informing all personnel to keep a lookout for Miyu and Yori. It's instantly transmitted to all Corp. soldiers and droids with pictures included. They are now considered extremely dangerous and the corporations top priority, to be terminated on sight.

The riots are becoming exceedingly dangerous as civilians and soldiers attack one another. Behind a nearby wall where a building once stood, Miyu watches a group of soldiers and waits for her chance to cross the street. While the soldiers are distracted with some rioters she quickly runs across the open terrain to a building on the other side of the street.

A light shines through the dust from above, sweeping the area. Just before Miyu is hidden from view, the Talon overhead spots her. They send word of her location through the network as she ducks into the building for cover.

Many nearby soldiers and DX-39 droids begin to converge on her location. She quietly traverses through the building when suddenly a barrage of gunfire tears through the walls. She increases her pace, quickly moving through the building looking for a way out.

Missiles blow holes in the walls and through one of these holes emerges a DX-39 followed by a group of soldiers. Miyu hides in the shadows and observes the soldiers from a room

116

tucked away at the end of a narrow hallway.

The soldiers fan out, combing the area for her while the DX-39 stays in the bigger room by the hole in the wall and scans its surroundings. The group of soldiers cautiously move down the hall toward her, separated from her by only several meters as they check each connected room.

She waits silently just inside to the left of the door. As one of the soldiers begins to enter, leading with his gun, she grabs it then hits him with such force he flies back down the hall leaving his gun in her hand. She quickly fills the hall with bullets, hitting several soldiers while others dive for cover.

The DX-39 turns and launches a missile down the hall while the rest of the soldiers return fire. She ducks back into the room as the missile whizzes by and slams into the wall on the far side of the room. The firing stops for a brief moment, an eerie silence envelops the area.

A soldier, who jumped into the room closest to Miyu to avoid the danger, listens intently for any sign of life coming from the other side of the wall. He turns on his thermal vision just in time to see Miyu burst through the wall and render him unconscious.

She quickly ducks back into the room from which she came while everyone opens fire on that location, bullets tear through the walls. While the soldiers are distracted with their fire concentrated to the left, she quickly darts toward the hole the DX-39's missile created in the wall on the far side of the room and leaps through it into the alley.

As her feet hit the ground she glances up and notices the searchlight of a Talon banking around the corner of the building. It immediately sends bullets flying all around her as she rushes toward safety at the far end of the alley.

As she rounds the corner to the right at the end of the alley, she is greeted by the blinding light of another Talon shining in her face. She quickly changes direction and runs to the left across the street as bullets trail her foot steps. The Talon lets two missiles fly. She leaps over a railing on the other side of the street and slides down an embankment into a drainage ditch as the missiles explode overhead.

118

She hits the ground running and makes haste toward the safety of a drainage tunnel as the pursuing units hover overhead continuing their barrage. The uncertainty of the dark, damp tunnel lies before her. Bright lights of the Talons trail behind. She weighs her options and realizes it is too dangerous to go back. She decides to push on, deeper into the darkness.

Yori makes his way across the rugged and hostile terrain toward the fallen space station. From a higher vantage point on top of a broken building, Yori notices a group of soldiers surrounding a few civilians beneath him. Knowing they are outnumbered and outgunned the civilians prepare to be executed, closing their eyes tightly, awaiting the inevitable.

"Aim," the squad leader says as the soldiers prepare to fire.

Yori leaps from the building landing behind the closest soldier, slicing his back open with his sword in the process. The soldier to the right has just enough time to look in Yori's direction before his head is lobbed off. In the same motion, Yori runs his blade through the next closest soldiers' chest.

"Fire!" the squad leader yells as he points at Yori. The remaining soldiers train their sights on Yori.

Yori ducks behind the soldier still stuck to his sword as they pump numerous rounds into his back. Using the soldiers gun Yori returns fire, putting down the rest of the surrounding troops. Cringing in fear, not noticing the chaos that took place around them, the civilians open their eyes to see Yori standing before them over the soldiers corpses.

"Thank you," one manages to say after a moment.

"Don't mention it," Yori says. "Get out of here while you still can."

Yori watches as the civilians run off in the distance. As he turns around to head toward the station a genetically enhanced agent catches him by surprise with a backhand to the face. He follows up with a kick to the chest sending Yori tumbling over a corpse, landing on his back, then rolling to his stomach. Yori places his palms on the ground and pushes himself up as he looks up at the agent confidently walking toward him.

The agent readies his weapon and prepares to shoot, when suddenly a mutated beast that emerged from the station lunges off some nearby rubble from the left and slams into him knocking him down. Looking on at the viciousness of the mutant brutally murdering his attacker, Yori decides to seize the opportunity and flee the scene, quickly climbing over the rubble to the left. On top of the rubble Yori realizes the true severity of the situation as he sees hundreds of mutants emerging from the station, savagely attacking soldiers and civilians alike.

Miyu progresses deeper into the dimly lit tunnel. Lights are strung up few and far between leaving much of the tunnel in darkness. She hears a sound all too familiar in the shadows in front of her stopping her in her tracks, sending shivers down her spine. Squinting her eyes she can make out a faint outline of a figure in the distance. Suddenly the visions in her dreams become reality, she finds herself face to face with a mutated beast as it steps out of the shadows into the light.

Facing her fears she prepares to fight as it snarls at her, moving ever closer. It quickly lunges at her just as the one in her dream. She falls to her back and uses its momentum against it, planting her foot in its chest, throwing it over her through the air.

Quickly back on her feet she turns to face it as it swipes its claws at her in a flurry of attacks. She jumps back and dodges the first swing, then leans back and to the right dodging the second.

She catches its arm on the third attempt with her right hand and breaks it at the elbow with an uppercut from her left hand. The beast lets out a blood curdling roar from the pain, yet doesn't miss a beat as it continues to attack.

Swiping at her with its other arm, its claws tear through the flesh of her shoulder as she tries to dodge the attack. She ducks under the next swing and uppercuts the beast with such force it flies off the ground and slams into the ceiling of the tunnel before splashing down in the ankle high water on the floor.

The impact cracks the ceiling and small chunks of rubble fall on top of the beast. With the threat eliminated she begins to head further down the tunnel only to be confronted by more beasts, this time three at once. She jumps to the side as the first one lunges at her and successfully dodges its attack.

As the second one leaps at her she punches it out of mid

air sending it hurtling into the wall on the opposite side of the tunnel. She leans back dodging the swipe of the third beast's deadly claws, then leans left dodging its second attack.

She ducks under its third swipe, then spins and kicks it in the chest knocking it back. The beast that attacked first comes at her again from the other side. She does a back hand spring dodging its volley of swipes, then punches it in the face breaking its neck and shattering its skull, almost knocking its head clear off its body.

The second beast attacks again with a quickness, swinging at her with its right arm. She puts both her forearms up to block the attack, elbows the beast in the face with her left arm, then catapults off the ground, powering her knee into its face.

The force of her attack shatters almost every bone in its face as the beast falls to the ground incapacitated. As she lands, the third beast leaps at her again. She quickly counters, doing a back flip while kicking it in mid air. When she lands she leaps toward the beast, putting all her might into her attack she punches it in the chest before it hits the ground. She powers her arm clean through the beast's torso, ejecting its innards out its back.

Just as she thinks the worst is over she hears a rumbling coming through the tunnel. She turns and glances down the tunnel looking on in horror, taking a deep breath in as her eyes widen. A sheer look of terror consumes her face, quite possibly a hundred more beasts advance toward her in the reflection of her fear gaped eyes. They flow like water through the tunnel, some of which are crawling on the walls and ceiling.

On the surface above soldiers fire frantically, trying to keep up with the agility of the mutants as they quickly hop about. Sounds of gunshots, agony and snarling beasts echo through the surroundings as Yori works his way closer to the station. He manages to sneak past most of the carnage, keeping his distance from the sounds of commotion. He is soon surrounded by what's left of a building on one side and a mound of rubble on the other as he cautiously traverses through the area.

In front of him, on the other side of the mound of rubble, he hears something climbing up. He slowly grasps his hand around the hilt of his sword and listens intently.

Slowly emerging on top of the rubble stands a mutant looking down on him, letting out a low growl. He stands still, ready to strike as he patiently awaits the beasts next move. The beast leaps from the high ground and lands on top of Yori knocking him on his back.

His sword, partially sheathed, rests in the beasts jaws keeping it from biting his face as it hovers over him. He struggles with the sheer power of the intimidating beast as saliva drips from its mouth. He quickly unsheathes his sword cutting one side of the beasts mouth, then kicks it off of him and gets back on his feet. The beast regains its composure then leaps through the air at him. He rolls forward under the beast, dodging its attack.

The beast turns around and takes a swing at him with its razor sharp claws. Yori flips over its arm just as he did before with Brock's chain and lobs its arm off with his blade. Upon landing, as the beast roars in pain, he plunges his blade into its mouth. His blade sticks into the roof of the beasts mouth, through its brain and out the back of its skull. The beast falls to the ground and Yori pulls his blade free, then continues on.

Back in the tunnels below, Miyu struggles with the

overwhelming amount of mutants rushing toward her. As strong and agile as she is, she is giving it all she has to fend off the countless beasts. She tears through the first twenty or so with blazing speed.

As they become more condensed they begin to gain the upper hand with their sheer numbers. Within a few seconds she loses control of the situation and they begin to pile on top of her.

Under their weight, shrouded by piercing claws and snarling jaws, she falls to her knees in exhaustion. She closes her eyes in this time of darkness and desperation, deep within her thoughts she begins to awaken her true power. In her minds eye she hovers above the beasts, seeing the surroundings as if she is in some sort of out of body experience just as before.

She feels a sudden surge of energy flowing through her, fueled by her anger toward the corporation and the loss of her grandfather. Her fears of the beasts melt away and a calming sense of serenity comes over her as she opens her eyes.

Just by merely thinking it, she stands up and a sphere of

telekinetic shock waves emanates from her, launching the creatures off of her and devastating everything within a ten meter radius. The tunnel ceiling and walls crumble under the force of the blast.

Free from their clutches she begins her attack on the remaining mutants, moving faster than before with heightened awareness and strength. She progresses down the tunnel easily defeating any beast left standing in her way as they cannot match her speed, agility and power. She finishes off the last of them and does not waste a moment to glance back at the countless bodies left in her wake as she heads down the tunnel toward the station.

CHAPTER IX.

BATTLE OF THE GODS.

Vincent struggles to his feet, battered and shaken from the colossal impact. He makes his way through the devastated surroundings and enters a section of the station that is extremely mangled. Looking through the massive hole that is gouged from the structure he sees a glimpse, from a distance, of the carnage that ensues outside across the city. Sensing that he is not alone he speaks, breaking the tension.

"Magnificent isn't it?" he says. "Look at the destruction... smell the fear... Have you come to face your fears? Don't be afraid."

Miyu steps out from the shadows behind him.

"I am not afraid," she says. "I'm here to put an end to this."

"And how pray tell do you plan to do that?" He says with a smirk.

"I'm going to kill you," she quickly answers.

"Ha ha ha! Your efforts are in vain," he says as he turns to face her. "I cannot be killed."

"We'll see about that," she says.

"You would fight against your creator? You will regret that decision," he says. "I created you and I can destroy you. Your plan to save Kenji has failed, do you think this will be any different?"

Her eyes fill with rage as she recalls the past events with Kenji and the mutants.

"You really are an incredible specimen... Join me," he says. "Think of the possibilities."

"I'd rather die," she says.

"So be it," he says.

He quickly leaps at her, striking with a flurry of attacks. She manages to dodge and block all of his attacks, but his speed is alarming. She finishes his wave of attacks by countering with an attack of her own that knocks him back a few meters. He pauses for a brief moment and regains his bearings.

"Impressive," he says. "Quite impressive."

Before he can get another word in Miyu quickly jumps into action with her own offensive. He matches her speed, quickly dodging most of her attacks. They both trade blows back and forth severely beating one another.

Just outside, amidst the violence and chaos, Yori sneaks past some soldiers busy fighting off mutants and enters the wreckage through a small hole in a mangled section of the station. Inside it is difficult to distinguish what is the station and what is the buildings that not long ago were fully erect in the same location.

Yori hears commotion coming from around the corner up ahead. The noise of gunfire and vicious snarls alerts him. He slowly approaches and peaks around the corner. He sees a small group of soldiers that has fallen back into the safety of the wreckage, using the more narrow surroundings to their advantage. They are using the narrow layout of a corridor to bottleneck a group of mutants into their onslaught of gunfire.

Trying not to draw too much attention to himself, Yori sits back and watches the conflict from a distance. Bullets rip through the mutants, yet they still manage to advance on the soldiers and slaughter several of them in the process. Finally, when the confrontation has ended only two agents remain.

The agents begin to relax a little now that the immediate threat is presumably eliminated. Yori grasps his sword, one hand on the sheath, the other firmly grips the hilt. Yori comes running down the hall while unsheathing his blade as the agents turn and look at one another.

In one swift motion he flip kicks one of them in the chest sending him into the wall behind them, then lobs off the other one's head. Just as quickly as the agent hits the wall, Yori's blade penetrates through his throat and sticks him to the wall. Yori doesn't waste a moment, he pulls his sword free and continues his search for Miyu.

Miyu and Vincent continue to engage one another in an

intense battle with lightning speed. The fight continues for about a minute as each of them get quite a few shots in on one another. Vincent gets the upper hand and delivers a powerful blow that sends Miyu tumbling to the ground.

"Kenji would have been disappointed," he says, slowly walking toward her as she struggles to her feet. "No more holding back, it is time you felt my true power!"

As she regains her balance his words build hatred and anger deep within her. He quickly lunges at her with a powerful punch only to be stopped in his tracks. With her eyes closed she has caught his fist in front of her face, Vincent is stunned. A strange energy radiates from her as her hair and some surrounding debris begin to float.

Vincent looks on in disbelief, having never seen or even imagined such power. She opens her eyes and a shock wave of surging energy explodes from her, more powerful than in the tunnel before. Vincent is hurtled through the air into a pile of clutter on the other side of the room.

The use of such power has taken its toll on her. Exhausted, she collapses to her knees on the floor. Vincent slowly climbs out of the pile and staggers for a moment, shaken by the attack.

"Absolutely amazing!" he says. "I've never dreamed of such power. You are indeed magnificent, it's unfortunate that I have to kill you now."

Just as she manages to get back on her feet he backhands her in the face knocking her back, she rolls to a stop a good distance from him. As Vincent arrogantly walks toward her he hears the thunk of metal hitting the floor and rolling in his direction. He turns around and looks down to see a pulse grenade. It explodes and blows him back through the air.

"I'm beginning to get annoyed with your toys," he says.

Shaken, he regains his footing and notices Yori at the far end of the room.

"I admire your courage," he says. "Stepping into the belly of the beast. Facing certain death, for what?"

Yori glances at Miyu as she begins to regain consciousness. Vincent looks over his shoulder at her.

"She *is* extraordinary isn't she?" he says. "Are you willing to sacrifice your life for her?"

Without hesitation Yori launches a throwing knife that lodges into Vincent's chest. He calmly looks down at the blade sticking out of him and pulls it out. Vincent cynically smiles then rushes at Yori, who throws four more knives at him, all hitting their mark. The knives don't seem to phase him as Vincent continues his attack with the blades still sticking into his flesh.

Yori anticipates his actions and manages to match his speed, dodging his flurry of attacks with amazing agility. Yori clenches his sword tightly, still sheathed, looking for an opportunity to strike.

Vincent throws a hay maker swing and Yori finally sees his chance. He performs an aerial somersault over his arm; in one quick motion he reveals his blade, slices Vincent's forearm in half while upside down, then sheathes his blade while still in the air.

Just as his feet hit the ground, Vincent backhands him with his freshly severed nub of an arm. Yori gets thrown through the air at least five meters before he hits the ground.

"Not bad," Vincent says as he picks up his severed arm and holds it in place.

"I'm really going to enjoy tearing you apart," he says as his arm reattaches and he makes a fist.

He pulls out the knives still lodged in his flesh and over confidently walks toward Yori as he gets to his feet.

"I expected more of a fight from you," he says. "It's pathetic really... I'm disappointed."

He grabs Yori and knees him, lifting him off the ground. He grabs Yori by the throat and lifts him up in the air, then punches him in the chest knocking him across the room.

Vincent hears the hum of a ships engines behind him. As he turns around he sees two missiles flying toward him. He bats one out of the air with his hand and it flies into a wall a short distance away. As it explodes the other hits the ground in front of him and explodes, blowing him back as it singes his flesh.

The missiles came from Marty's ship. It maneuvers through the gouge in the wall and turns around, hovering in place as the rear bay doors open. Using all her effort, Miyu begins to make her way toward the ship and Brock hops out from the cargo bay to help her along.

CHAPTER X.

NEW HORIZONS.

*Y*ori struggles to his feet as Vincent climbs out of the rubble. His wounds begin to heal themselves as he advances toward Yori. Brock helps Miyu on board the ship, then quickly mans the massive fully auto gun bolted to the lower bay door.

He unleashes a hail of bullets that whiz past Yori as he struggles to reach the ship. They penetrate Vincent's flesh, gouging chunks from his body and slowing him down.

"Come on Yori!" Brock shouts, still blasting away.

In the cockpit Elisa picks up some disturbing activity on the sensors, several Talons are rapidly approaching their location.

"We got company," she says frantically.

"Shit!" Marty says looking at the sensors.

Back in the cargo bay Brock hears them over the com.

"We're out of time," Marty says.

Struggling through the pain, Yori begins to run toward the ship.

"Come on," Brock says anxiously.

"We gotta go now!" Marty says over the com.

"Punch it!" he says to Elisa and she slams the throttle.

Yori is running as fast as he can to make it on board as the ship begins to pull away. The ground under his feet quickly runs out and he leaps for the ship. Miyu stretches out her hand, reaching out of the ship from the edge of the lower bay door, trying to catch him.

She looks deep into his eyes and he into hers, their fingertips graze one another. Her heart sinks in disbelief as she watches him, in what seems to be slow motion, fall further away as the ship rapidly picks up speed then banks around a building. She doesn't blink or take her eyes off of him until he is no longer in sight.

"Betsy, how many lifeforms are on board?" Marty says to his ship.

"Six," the ship responds in a female voice.

Two Talons come around the buildings into view behind them and they give chase. Brock stands at the gun, frozen in place for a moment, trying to comprehend what just happened. A third Talon soon joins the others in the pursuit.

The Talons fire a few rounds in their direction as the ship banks and sways trying to shake them off. Miyu ducks back into the ship and straps herself into a bench-like chair on the side wall of the cargo bay as a few rounds clank off the ship close by. The noise from the shots snaps Brock out of his daze. He furiously opens fire on the Talons and hits one of the ships engines, blowing it out of the sky.

"Hang on back there!" Elisa shouts over the com.

Brock quickly straps in as he continues to fire, knowing when Elisa says something like that she means business. The remaining two Talons take evasive action while trying to stay on the ships tail. Elisa, being the excellent pilot that she is, weaves through the buildings with blinding speed and nerves of steel. As she rounds a building she notices two more Talons up ahead hovering in place, ready to strike.

She quickly fires a few missiles at them just before they open fire, then she slams the stick forward sending the ship into a nose dive toward the ground. Chloe raises up off the floor, hair standing on end as she lets out a squeal while floating in the air from the rapid descent of the ship. The gunfire from the Talons barely misses them and shreds through one of the ships chasing them. Her missiles connect with the ship on the left, causing it to bank into the other one hovering next to it.

Elisa flies Betsy underneath the two ships as they plummet to the ground and barely miss the last Talon chasing them as it weaves through the falling debris. Elisa pulls up, flying dangerously close to the ground, banking violently to avoid hitting obstructions. She notices a tunnel up ahead and fearlessly flies full speed into it and the last remaining Talon follows without hesitation.

With very little room to maneuver, the Talon seizes the

140

opportunity and fires a missile at them. Alarms sound in the cockpit warning them of the incoming threat. Elisa banks slightly to the right at the last second raising the port side of the ship just enough for the missile to pass under it.

The missile flies ahead of them, hits the wall up ahead and explodes, sending chunks of rubble tumbling in front of them. Elisa banks the opposite direction, causing the port side of the ship to drop just under the rubble as they fly by. The Talon behind them gets lucky enough to miss the big chunks as it flies through the dust and debris, smaller chunks clank off the ship and crack the canopy.

The pilot regains visibility past the debris and notices the end of the tunnel up ahead, yet the ship he was chasing is no longer in sight. When Elisa exited the tunnel she quickly raised her altitude, banked to the left and spun the ship two hundred seventy degrees before coming to a halt. She lies in wait hovering in place, training her sights on the tunnel's exit. As the Talon exits the tunnel the pilot looks around scanning the area, noticing them a moment too late. She opens fire shredding his ship to pieces, it bursts into smoke and flame as it banks into the ground.

"I didn't know this ship could handle like that," Marty says.

"Me either," Elisa says with a smile.

"Let's head back to the shop," he says. "We need to pick up some supplies, and I need a new pair of shorts."

"Supplies? For what?" she asks.

"After all the shit we've caused we're gonna have to lay low for a while," he says, then pauses for a moment. "That was close... A little too close. Ya did good kiddo! Everyone's alright thanks to you. Let's go get those supplies, I'm gonna let everyone know we're headed to Mars."

Elisa sets course for the shop, anxious to see Mars for the first time. Back in the cargo bay area Brock is shutting the bay doors as Marty walks in.

"Alright everyone listen up—" he says.

Frozen in mid sentence he realizes that Yori isn't on board the ship.

"Where's Yori?" he says.

Miyu sits silently in shock, uncertain of what the future brings.

"He didn't make it," Brock says, still in disbelief.

Many seconds of uncomfortable silence tick by as Marty tries to make sense of the situation.

"Betsy, how many lifeforms are on board?" he says.

"Six," the ship replies with the same number as before.

Marty counts everyone on board in his head; Elisa, Brock, Miyu, himself and Elisa's cat Chloe makes five. Where is this sixth entity the ship is registering? Miyu glances at Kenji's body strapped to the bench on the other side of the bay, then looks at Marty with a confused look on her face as tears roll down her cheeks.

She is completely devastated from recently losing the two people she cares about most in such a small amount of time. Unbeknownst to her, the sixth life form is actually inside her. Due to her unique abilities the embryo of Yori and her child, already vastly accelerated, is rapidly growing within her womb.

THE END.

This book is also available in digital format on Amazon Kindle Store and Google Play. I hope you enjoyed the story. Visit the Dailey Worx facebook page to keep up with the latest news on events, upcoming books and for more information here:

http://www.facebook.com/DaileyWorx

Printed by CreateSpace

Amazon, Google Play, Facebook and CreateSpace are copyrights of their respective companies.

www.ingramcontent.com/pod-product-compliance
Lightning Source LLC
Chambersburg PA
CBHW070936130626
46555CB00001B/459